430

FANTASTIC 4 ®

RISE OF THE SILVER SURFER

FANTASTIC 4®
RISE OF THE SILVER SURFER

A Novelization by Daniel Josephs
Based on the Motion Picture
Screenplay by Don Payne
Story by Mark Frost

POCKET STAR BOOKS

New York London Toronto Sydney

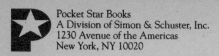

Pocket Star Books
A Division of Simon & Schuster, Inc.
1230 Avenue of the Americas
New York, NY 10020

This book is a work of fiction. Names, characters, places, and incidents are
products of the author's imagination or are used fictitiously. Any resemblance
to actual events or locales or persons, living or dead, is entirely coincidental.

First Pocket Star Books paperback edition May 2007

POCKET STAR BOOKS and colophon are registered trademarks of
Simon & Schuster, Inc.

For information regarding special discounts for bulk purchases,
please contact Simon & Schuster Special Sales at 1-800-456-6798
or business@simonandschuster.com

Manufactured in the United States of America

10 9 8 7 6 5 4 3 2 1

ISBN 13: 978-1-4165-4809-6
ISBN 10:   1-4165-4809-2

FANTASTIC 4 ®

RISE OF THE
SILVER SURFER

PROLOGUE

THE PLANET SAT SILENTLY, WAITING, ROTATING IN AN inky sea of black space . . . turning slowly, even at a thousand miles per hour, revealing its skin of deep blues interrupted only by small patches of greens and browns. For millennia, the planet existed silently, orbiting near other, equally silent planets—their only companions the distant stars, small specks of silver and dust that cast an inconsistent glow, bathing the endless expanse of deep black with uneven light. In the soundless sea of space, the planet's majesty took on an unshakable feeling of solitude, even loneliness.

Until now.

In the far corner of the heavens, a crack appeared. At first it seemed no larger than a wayward spark, an inconsequential shard of silver leaking out from a broken, faraway star.

The crack grew larger as it moved through space with a speed never before seen so close to this silent group of planets. It zoomed closer and closer to the slowly turning blue globe, as if drawn by its calming colors, leaving a bright, radiant dust in its wake. As the object increased its speed, the dust scattered, and a thundering shock wave of cosmic energy followed. Waves of red and orange bent and slithered like snakes, rippling across the endless blackness—a stunning display, a violent burst of color and fingers of crackling light.

The object continued forward, heading straight for the large planet below.

It reached the outer skin of the Earth's atmosphere and the results were instantaneous. More energy burned from the object as a fierce electrical storm formed behind it, unleashing torrents of lightning and more fingers of rippling energy. For a brief moment, the vast emptiness of space was no longer dark, no longer silent, no longer cold and quiet.

The first light of dawn calmly awakened the small Japanese village, the blue sky opening like a flower. Three men gathered their fishing gear and stowed it in the old wooden boat, carefully making their way out into the tranquil waters of the lake.

They attempted to remain noiseless so as not to startle the fish, using small oars and swift strokes instead of the loud onboard engine. Generations of their family had fished these waters, and the lessons had been passed down eagerly: *Stay quiet; be patient; let the good things find you.* For years, nothing had changed—not the route of the fishermen, or the baits on the line, or the bamboo poles cherished for their strength and lightness. The view was the same as it always had been: the expanse of calm water and the morning light playing upon the slight waves, giving the entire lake a shimmer.

It was the serenity of this lake that the fishermen relished almost as much as the sustenance it provided. A good haul could feed the village for days. But the sight of the lake, the air fresh and clean and soft, filled them for much longer.

The lead fisherman moved quickly to the front of the boat, letting his two brothers continue to row in the rear. As the eldest, it was his duty to lead them to the deepest part of the lake, where the biggest fish swam. His eyes narrowed as he tried to look past the glare of the sun for the telltale signs: a ripple in the water, a moving light, a small wave.

The lead fisherman kept a tight grip on either side of the wooden boat, a sudden intensity in his eyes the only sign of his trepidation. Truth be told, for all his competence and ease with the fish, there was one thing he was still afraid of: the water. He did not know how to swim.

This fear of water had always haunted him, especially during his younger years, when he was eager to prove himself as a brave provider for his village. Some nights, back then, he'd wake up bathed in sweat from the familiar nightmare: the tossing wave, the rocking and shaking of the boat, which eventually pitched him over into the deep, cold water of the lake. He felt the dampness over him like a weight as the water seeped into his bones, pulling him down to its icy depths. His mind always let him see that final image of his brothers, their mouths moving quickly, arms outstretched as they tried to reach their flailing, incompetent sibling, in their eyes a mixture of fear and disappointment, as if they, too, had been expecting this all along. The dream always ended just after he tried to open his mouth to scream, to say good-bye, the water filling him with the overwhelming taste of death.

The fisherman shook his head to wipe the remnants of the dream from his mind, letting the cool lake air wash over his face. *Stupid fear, childish fear*, he admonished himself. *Such is the imagination of the young.* He smiled at himself, feeling foolish, as he leaned over the moving water.

Out of the corner his eye, he saw it: a flash, a darting of light. Was it something deep below? He could not tell; it went by too rapidly. *What type of fish could move that fast?*

The fisherman, staring deep into the water, could not see his two brothers clasping their oars as they looked above them, high into the clear blue sky. Nor could the fisherman guess that what he saw on the water was only a reflection of something moving above him, rather than below. The silver blur disappeared as quickly as it had appeared.

Suddenly the boat began to pitch as a loud, violent shock wave swept over the entire body of water. The fishermen grabbed on to the sides of the old wooden boat, their voices rising, fear clouding their thoughts. The boat tipped and fell, as the lake was now a torrent of waves, tossing the vessel about like a toy. Cold water sloshed into the boat, seeping through the clothes of the terrified fishermen, their eyes stinging. A loud rumble grew in their ears and in their terror they envisioned the boat tearing itself apart. The noise escalated to a crescendo, loud, booming, crackling, the sound turning almost physical as it blew across their clothes like the wind.

The boat suddenly lurched to a halt, the wood creaking and shrieking as loud as those it carried. The men in the back held on as tightly as they could, the wood splintering in their callused, trembling hands, drawing blood across their fingers and palms.

But the eldest fisherman, the one in the front, had nothing to hold on to but the narrow bow, where the wood was thinnest, where it was already cracked and falling into the water. The sudden movement of the boat left him no choice but to submit. And just as the shockwave reached its loudest point, he released his grip and was thrown over the side of the vessel into the rapidly turning water.

The fisherman was once again in his childhood dream. He saw the violently rocking boat, tasted the fear in his mouth, heard the sounds he told himself existed only in his head. And, as always, he saw his brothers reaching out to him, their hands stained this time with their own blood. His body shut down and he prepared to feel the icy water take him over, to be dragged deep down to a cold grave. His mind caved in fear as he realized that his nightmare was made real.

Suddenly, all was silent. The shock wave receded, the colors disappeared, and the sky returned to its pale blue hue. He could not hear the rushing water, could not feel it taking him over like a heavy blanket, could not hear his brothers crying his name. He could not hear anything. Raising his hands to his face, he saw they were intact, and dry. He lay beside his family's boat, not drowning.

He had fallen onto a sea of solid rock.

Half a world away, a tiny European village sat nestled amid thick woods and trees. Isolated and silent, the village shared the same view as Earth: deep, inky night; silver specks of stars; a pale, lonely moon. The village was undisturbed—there was not even a wind to rustle the thick leaves on the trees in the dense forest. The dirt, untouched for years, lay heavily on the ground, as if sleeping deeply. Large stones marked a pathway up to an old mansion, its heavy facade as silent as the forest that surrounded it. The mansion was as old as the village itself, held over from a time long forgotten, when small groups of nomads roamed through this countryside aided only by the light of burning torches.

The main room of the mansion housed dozens of large, dusty crates. The moon shone through a large bay window, giving just enough light to show the small rats and vermin lurking in the corners, hunger serving as their only companion. The only sign of modernity in the room was the now faded ink used to stamp the large wooden crates with the words VON DOOM ENTERPRISES. In the center of the room stood the largest crate, a rectangle nearly seven feet high. Its nails long had ago lost their sheen, giving way to rust and dust.

Overhead, among the dim stars, a small brightness appeared, growing stronger as it passed over the village. The trees of the forest began to shudder and shake, and the dirt on the ground moved for the first time in years. Strong winds blew the carpet of the forest around, large pieces of rubble slapping the trunks of the trees in violent gusts. A solitary silver object passed through the sky, illuminating the tops of the thick trees for only a moment. With loud bursts the silver object was gone, leaving a cloud of thick, radiant energy that began to fall gently to the ground. The glowing rain covered the entire village, bathing the forests and the mansion in its shining hue. The energy moved like water over the old stone walls of the mansion.

The iridescent wave fell through the shoddy roof and into each room of the mansion, lighting the old structure. Rats scurried to the farthest corners of the large main room, running past the wooden crates, fearful of the incandescence moving over the space, their eyes glowing red. The curtain of energy spilled quickly over the largest crate in the room, covering it entirely. Wooden slats rattled and shook, the rusty nails once again taking on a silver sheen. Inside the crate, a large statue made of solid metal was bathed in the energy, illuminated by the moving, shimmering light. The dull, aged metal took on a new shine, its limbs and torso glowing as if they'd been scrubbed by the powerful energy.

The eyes of the statue opened suddenly, burning with a sadistic energy all their own.

1

SUSAN STORM STOOD STARING AT THE COMMERCIAL JET on the airport tarmac, its large belly reflecting the afternoon sun with a powerful glare. The engines of the jet were silent, at least to her, as she watched several figures on the ground loading luggage and moving around the jet with ear protectors fastened tightly to their heads. She lingered on the activity on the ground, the scurrying and the action that she was not a part of, grateful to have something else to focus on. Often she begged her fiancé, Reed Richards, to find some other way for them to travel, some other way that didn't make her feel so exposed, so *seen.*

Susan blinked away the darker thoughts, turning from the window of the airport terminal and letting her eyes become readjusted from the glare of the afternoon light. Inside the terminal at LAX, all silence was obliterated. A crowd had immediately formed around her and her family as soon as they'd arrived at the gate to wait for their flight back to New York. She tried to block out the squeals of delight from the onlookers, the rush of the crowd that usually seemed to suck all the oxygen out of the room. She attempted to refocus, to ignore the voices gathering around them, the clicking of cell phone cameras, the murmurs and whispers that stuck to her skin so quickly that sometimes she could feel them before she heard them. Before the strange hands touched her arms or shoulders. One time, there'd been a tug on her long blond hair.

Is that them? Oh my God, I can't believe it. They look so different up close. What the hell is she wearing? Do you think she's pregnant?

Of all the things that had changed about Sue's life since the cosmic storm—the storm that altered her DNA and gave her powers beyond anything imaginable, powers that drew her back into the world of Reed Richards, powers that led to the defeat and death of Victor Von Doom—it was being thrown into the public eye that remained the most difficult. She disliked it intensely: the constant staring, the roving cameras that followed them wherever they went, the intense scrutiny that came with such attention.

For the most part, she had accepted the fate that had befallen them. If they suddenly had powers that could be useful to mankind, so be it. She was willing to share them and to do her part to make the world a safer place. She wasn't haunted by the changes in her life, the way she suspected Ben Grimm might be; nor did she relish the limelight the way her younger brother, Johnny, did. And Reed? He barely noticed anything beyond a book or his PDA. With the outside world rushing so violently into their private space, she often wondered how he could remain so clueless to the million different ways their lives had been invaded.

Sue felt a small weight in her chest. She rubbed her hands together, staring at the slim band of silver around her finger, trying to dismiss her cranky, cynical thoughts. She knew these weren't the musings of a hero, or of someone grateful for her life and upcoming wedding, or of someone even the least bit fantastic. It happened to her sometimes, when the crush of it all became a bit too much, when she'd retreat inside herself, if only to get a break from the attention and the spotlight. But the thoughts were beginning to stay with her for longer periods of time, and even her power of invisibility, her ability to disappear from their sight, could not make them go away.

She walked over to where Reed and Ben were sitting, waiting for the flight. The airport lounge was large and quite generic, she felt, for such a metropolitan city. They had bypassed the coffee bars and newsstands, hoping to lose the seemingly necessary crowds. But they were unavoidable. She noticed the people all around them and made a note to speak to Reed again about finding a less public way to travel. An overhead television caught her attention as she noticed the people in the waiting area staring intently at the talking flat screen.

The TV showed a typical blond anchorwoman with too many teeth talking about Susan and the team. The anchorwoman stared blankly into space and spoke: "It's being called the wedding of the century. Reed Richards and Susan Storm, also known as Mr. Fantastic and the Invisible Woman, will try again to tie the knot three days from now at a private ceremony at the newly remodeled Baxter Building. They're hoping the fifth time's the charm, as the unlucky couple has repeatedly had to reschedule the event due to 'unforeseen circumstances.' But even the delays haven't dampened the enthusiasm of the couple's fans."

Susan cringed at the thought of her personal life being so vividly displayed for the world to see. She and Reed were in love. It wasn't their fault that things kept intruding on their wedding plans. It wasn't like they were hesitant or filled with doubt, was it? She turned her attention back to the television screen, which now panned over a crowd of people. It seemed to her that these cable news shows always found the most extreme personalities to feature on their segments, making most of the public seem like freaks or extremists. This show was no different. The camera cut to rabidly cheering fans adorned with the now familiar and ubiquitous dark blue Fantastic Four T-shirts. Johnny had gone behind their backs again and struck a licensing deal to have their logo put on anything he could: clothing, hats, mugs, towels. Even a large lingerie manufacturer had been ready to make a deal before Sue put a stop to it. Her brother had no common sense, relying instead on his fiery ambition and, she hated to admit, his growing hunger for fame.

The news camera focused on a particularly ardent young couple, the man weighing about twice that of the woman next to him. He was wearing a blue T-shirt with a large number four on the chest and grabbed his young girlfriend for a particularly long, deep kiss, right on camera. When he came up for air he said, "My girlfriend and I are getting married on the same day. I even dyed my temples, right, sweetie?" He turned his large, round face to either side, showing the camera his gray temples. The young girl, with lipstick now smeared over her lips, was wearing a blue wedding dress also emblazoned with a number four.

Susan tried to dismiss the scene with a sense of humor. *At least* someone *is getting married*, she thought.

She made her way over to Reed and Ben. They were all dressed in regular clothes even though there was no way for them to blend in with the crowd. Johnny was standing a few feet from where they were sitting, surrounded, as always, by adoring fans. He was too busy signing autographs and having his picture taken to notice the others. A particularly loud group of screaming girls had just arrived on the scene, and Sue figured her brother would remain quite busy until before it was time to board their flight. Watching him interact with the public, it was easy to dismiss him as egocentric or selfish. But Susan knew her brother better than that, and for all his love of the spotlight and the fame and fortune that accompanied their high profile, he took his responsibilities very seriously. Wasn't he the first one to call this a *job*? She remembered him saying that, after their fight with Victor Von Doom. His powers, and his control over them, were growing exponentially. Susan, at that moment, almost envied how much her brother relished and was comfortable in the public eye.

Susan sat down next to Reed, who had his nose buried in some work, his long legs extended and resting on a suitcase. She smiled and rolled her eyes at Ben, who smiled back at her. Ben knew Reed almost as well as she did but was less frustrated by his distractions. She knew Ben had been working with Reed for years—nothing much surprised him about the absentminded professor Reed so often claimed to be.

Ben Grimm watched Susan take a seat next to Reed, her slight figure hardly moving the cheap airport seats at all. It took Ben five minutes to find a seat that might hold him, and he had to ease into it gently so as to not send it flying through the large windows onto the tarmac.

Ben turned his attention away from his friends and watched a group of young kids inch near him. It wasn't that long ago that kids—hell, most people—had blanched in fear at the sight of him. Not that that didn't still happen on occasion. But for the most part, the world seemed to have made its peace with his appearance. Ben struggled to do the same.

The lead boy was pushed ahead, farther toward Ben, while the others lingered a bit behind. The kid, dressed in a white T-shirt and jeans, held a sheet of paper in one hand and a pen in the other. His young eyes traveled from Ben's rocky face to his blue Brooklyn varsity jacket down to his two large, stony hands. The boy's face was a mixture of excitement and trepidation, his feet not leaving the ground even as the rest of his body tried to move forward. Ben smiled to himself. If only most of their fans were this hesitant, this polite. Sure would be a change of pace for Johnny.

Ben moved his hands away from the sides of the chair and extended them toward the kids. The others flinched back, but not the one with the pen. He stood firm, his eyes growing wide at seeing Ben's large rock hands, with their thick, significant fingers. Ben put his hands together, palms touching, and raised them to a height just above the heads of the children. He moved his hands together slowly, grinding them, the sound of falling rocks suddenly filling the air. Small pebbles fell into a pile before the smiling children. "Cool!" said the boy, before joining his friends in picking up their bounty from the floor of the terminal.

The commotion of children at his feet caused Reed Richards to finally look up from the papers and PDA in front of him. He raised an eyebrow at Ben and watched his old friend shrug his large, rock-hewn shoulders. The entire row of seats moved along with him. The motion caused some papers to fall from Reed's lap to the ground. Reed looked up at the television monitor as if noticing it for the first time, noting the continuing coverage of the energetic fans of the Fantastic Four.

The scene cut back to the anchorwoman in the news studio. "Look for hourly updates and complete live coverage of the big event right here on your Global News Network. Jim?"

The camera cut to a grinning, chisel-faced, sycophantic anchorman, who began hamming it up on cue. "Sounds *fantastic*, Jane."

"Unbelievable," Reed said to Ben. "Bizarre anomalies have been occurring all over the world, defying every known law of physics. And all the media want to know about is what china pattern Sue and I picked out."

"Which one *did* you pick out?" Ben asked, trying to lighten his friend's mood. "The blue with the little flowers? 'Cause I liked those."

Susan ignored Ben's attempt at humor and spoke directly to her fiancé. "It's happening again, isn't it?" A frown tarnished her beautiful face.

Reed spoke up quickly, noticing her unhappiness. "No! We're not postponing anything. Not this time. We're having a nice, safe ceremony at the Baxter Building. No interruptions." Reed went to take her hand but she pulled it away, either not wanting to be comforted or simply not believing him. Reed stretched his arm around her slim body and eventually grabbed her hand, the one with the silver band. He looked deep into her eyes. "This is going to be the wedding you've always dreamed of. And I am not going to let anything get in the way of that. Not even the mysterious transformation of matter at the subatomic level."

Susan couldn't help but smile as Reed released her from his tender grip. "Reed Richards, that's the most romantic thing you've ever said to me."

That's so sweet, Ben thought, genuinely happy for the two of them. Then he noticed Johnny coming their way. *Uh oh, here comes trouble.*

Sue was about to pull Reed in for a kiss when Johnny pushed in between them, placing his arms around the couple. "Which is pretty pathetic, when you think about it," he said, grinning from ear to ear.

Susan turned quickly, intending to admonish her brother for eavesdropping, but she was interrupted by a representative from the airline. The middle-aged man seemed fearful and excited at the same time. He spoke barely above a whisper, a voice probably used to placate those who were about to be inconvenienced. "Dr. Richards, I'm very sorry, but it seems we're overbooked in first class. We *do* have some seats available in coach, though."

Reed looked over at his fianceé, who simply sat back in her chair and folded her arms. Johnny had already left them and was walking across the room to another group of beautiful female admirers. Reed knew that Susan and her brother wouldn't complain too much. His concern was for Ben, who at times felt a bit insecure out among the public. Reed tried to speak to him, to offer his support, but he felt apprehensive about pushing the point too far. Ben Grimm, out of all of them, had changed the most after the cosmic storm. He couldn't turn his powers on and off the way the rest of them could; Ben had to live with them every hour of every day. So Reed felt it better to let Ben work it out in his own time, on his own schedule. Still, that didn't mean that Reed couldn't try to protect his best friend whenever he could.

Reed looked over at Ben, who remained busy with the children, oblivious to their situation. He was smiling, the corners of his rocky mouth turned up, holding two young boys on his shoulder for a picture.

Reed turned back to the airline representative. "That should be fine," he said.

Those words soon came back to haunt him.

The shining silver plane looked larger from the

outside than it actually was, and they all felt crowded in the close quarters. People with too much luggage jockeyed for position, trying to claim their seats, their overhead bins, and an extra blanket or two. The Fantastic Four's fame would prove useless in helping them get some extra storage space.

Susan was pushed from the side by a first-class passenger and longed to use her power to create a field around herself. The air inside the plane was already stifling, babies were crying, and the passengers were very aggressive in trying to map out some personal space. *At least they're finally not staring at us*, she thought, taking another elbow to the ribs.

Ben seemed to be reading her mind. "Reed, this is no way for super heroes to travel," he said from behind them, stuck between two chairs in the aisle. He worked his way free and set the two chairs rocking until their tray tables fell open.

"I'm working on it," Reed answered. He sighed. Susan patted him from behind as they moved down the crowded aisle.

Ben stopped a few rows later, having reached his designated seat. He turned to the two passengers already seated in his row, an empty seat between them. "That's my seat," Ben said, pointing a large finger at the narrow space. "Sorry." The man in the aisle stood to let Ben try to angle himself into the seat. The woman stayed quiet, hugging the window and arming herself with a thin airline pillow. Ben sighed.

A few rows back, Reed and Sue found their seats. At least they would be sitting together, Susan told herself, though she could tell from the look on Reed's face that he was worried about Ben. She loved that part of him, the part that tried to protect this group like a family. Reed struggled with trying to find some room in the overhead for their luggage. Of course, all the bins seemed to be full of overstuffed, too-large suitcases. It wasn't the first time that Susan considered traveling invisible, if only to save room in her luggage. She was about to pull Reed over and give him a kiss when her brother Johnny once again insinuated himself between them and spoke up. "Don't worry, guys," he said. "I'm working out an endorsement deal with an airline to get us a private jet." Johnny smiled his radiant grin and gave his sister a peck on the cheek, which burned a little.

She turned to him. "Another endorsement? Don't we have enough?" She gave her brother a familiar look of disappointment.

Johnny ignored his sister's look, as he usually did. "Never enough. Think about it." Seeing that he was getting nowhere with his sister, Johnny turned his attention to his soon-to-be brother-in-law. "Reed, I could help you subsidize more of your little inventions."

But Reed was having none of it. "No, thanks," was all he said in reply.

"No vision," Johnny muttered. "No one in this group has any vision. How can you be so inflexible?"

Just as Johnny finished the sentence, Reed's arm whizzed past his head and reached down the aisle, toward the back of the plane. Tired of struggling with their luggage, Reed found an empty overhead bin at the far end of the plane and put their bags there. After he was finished, Reed pulled his arm back quickly, moving the air just in front of Johnny.

"Just consider it," Johnny said, running his hand over his face. He blew a kiss to his sister. "I'll see you later."

Reed, who was just getting settled into his narrow seat, could not disguise his surprise. "Where are you going?"

Johnny looked back at them and made a face, his clean, clear features bunching up around the forehead, as if he smelled something foul. "I don't fly coach," Johnny said. He walked back up the aisle, which was significantly less crowded now that the seats were taken and the overhead bins were full.

Ben Grimm's large, rocky figure sat uncomfortably in the narrow seat. A flight attendant approached him, a sour look on her face. The attendant glanced at the passengers around Ben—a man practically sitting in the aisle and a woman crushed against the small window—and turned her attention back to the thing in the middle seat. "Sir, you'll have to buckle your seat belt before takeoff." She ran her hand over her perfect helmet of dark, shoulder-length hair.

Ben grunted loudly, startling the already startled passengers in his row. He turned from side to side, shaking all three seats, looking for the elusive seat belt. When he finally found it, he pulled the black belt up toward his lap. It barely reached past his leg. By now Ben was flustered, obviously unnerved by the extra attention and the disgusted look of the prickly airline attendant. Ben finally gripped the metal buckle of the belt and pulled, ripping it from the seat entirely. With a sheepish look on his rocky face, he handed the belt to the attendant. "Let's just forget about it this time," she said, her voice as cold as ice. She took the belt between her index finger and thumb, holding it as far away from herself as she could, and retreated back to her station.

Just then Johnny passed through the aisle and patted Ben on the back of his head. "Hang in there, big guy. It's only a five-hour flight."

Ben grunted again, this time as loud as he pleased. The light of the plane dimmed as it began to pull away from the gate. Ben tried to calm himself down, tried to shrink himself inside his bulky, rocky frame. He hated moments like this, times when his size and looks proved to be such a liability. *Guess it isn't all pictures with cheering kids*, he thought.

Ben glanced over to the window, past the woman

next to him, who seemed to want to disappear herself. In the late-afternoon sky Ben could see Johnny all aflame and flying beside the airplane. The sunlight glinted off the long silver wing, its angled shape resembling a surfboard. Johnny stayed just off the tip of the wing, waving enthusiastically to everyone on the flight.

Ben leaned back in his chair. It groaned and creaked in agony. On the inside, Ben did the same. "I hope it rains," he said.

The rain was coming down in sheets half a world away, in a small and remote European village. The coming night cooled the water as it blanketed the heavy trees and forests surrounding the mansion. Water leaked through the centuries-old stone, just as it always had, leaving drops and puddles throughout the damp manse, the chill of the air even colder than it was outside. The moon stayed high and hidden above the clouds of the storm as if it, too, wanted to steer clear of the decaying stone palace.

Inside the main room of the mansion, a spark of activity could be detected through the sheets of rain and occasional thunder. The man and the woman from the United States stood nervously in the darkened room, scarves tied thickly around their necks, their breath showing in the cold air. Both kept their thoughts to themselves, only half believing they were in this cold and damp place, so far from civilization. They had pried away the damp, thick side of the large rectangular crate and watched it fall heavily to the dusty stone floor. Inside the crate the solid metal statue stood silent, dark, and heavy with anticipation.

They cleared out enough room for the welder to work. In the thin light of a single bulb, the welder approached the statue. He looked over his task, the metal unpolished and unimpressive in the dirty, stingy light. His eyes followed a trail from its two feet up the thick legs to the brandished torso and, finally, to his mark. The faceplate dated back generations, yet looked modern in its shadowed malevolence. The eye slots were dark—*A good sign*, the welder thought—but the rigid, tarnished look of the metal told him this would be a difficult task. He didn't want to be here. He was freezing and hungry. He wasn't even sure if this would work. But jobs were scarce in this forgotten corner of the world, and God did he need the money.

With shaking hands, the young welder lit his acetylene torch. The flame burned true in the cold, inky room. It offered little heat, and the welder could see his breath as he let the air out of his lungs, gathering his calm. He raised the torch to the faceplate of the statue. He thought he saw a flicker of something, though it could have been a trick of the light. Suddenly a window blew open, startling everyone in the room. The welder jumped back and lowered his torch.

Just the wind. *Still a bad storm outside*, he thought to relax himself.

The welder let out another long breath and steadied his hands. He raised the torch to the faceplate again. He had no idea why anyone would want to take off the face of a statue, but he took the job, no questions asked. *Crazy Americans*, he thought to himself. *Taking everything from this country and changing it to their liking*.

The welder deftly brought his torch to the side of the faceplate, just below the statue's ear. The rigid metal gave way with surprising ease. The welder could tell by the brittle flaking that the metal hadn't seen heat in a while, having been locked away in the damp and dust for God knows how long.

When he brought the torch down the side of the neck, he smelled something burning. *This can't be right*, he thought to himself. *There's nothing in this damp tomb to burn*. But the smell grew stronger, wafting out from the statue and across the room. He looked back to see if the Americans had done something, perhaps lit a cigarette or candle. But they were standing as still as the statue, eyes wide and fearful, watching him. He could not quite place the smell, a rancid burning aroma, familiar and distinctive.

"Extraordinary," came the voice of the American woman from behind him.

As the welder turned back toward the statue he recognized the smell: that one time when he caught his finger in the torch. The smell of burning flesh.

He looked back at the faceplate just as the statue's eyes sprung open. He gasped, letting out his last breath. The arms of the statue came to life, one arm flashing up quickly to grab the welder's hand, the one holding the torch. The welder dropped the torch, its flame catching his pant leg on the way down.

The welder didn't look down as the familiar smell once again appeared in the room. His eyes were locked on the eyes of the statue, the one that had suddenly come to life, the one that now held him by the throat and raised him off the cold stone floor of the mansion. The last thing he heard was the voice of the American behind him. A man's voice. He thought he heard the man say "Hello, Victor" before he was thrown across the room, his neck shattering upon impact with the wall.

The statue put its hands together as if wiping dust from them. It locked eyes with the two others in the room. The man and woman shrunk away, shaking from the cold and something else.

The statue reached up and ripped away the faceplate, screaming. Bits of flesh hung loosely from the cold, hard metal.

2

MORNING BLOOMED BRIGHTLY ACROSS THE IMPRESSIVE Manhattan skyline, the rising sun shining on buildings that stood like sentinels. New York City was often called the greatest city in the world, and never did it seem more true than on such a resplendent morning, when the metal buildings contrasted beautifully against the pale blue sky and the deeper hues of the surrounding Hudson and East rivers, the city already awake and brimming with activity.

A bit north of Times Square, its streets already filled with men and women eager to start their day, just past the theater district of Broadway and its accompanying lane of eateries known as Restaurant Row, stood the newly remodeled Baxter Building. Situated slightly south of the great Central Park, the august building had seen its fair share of Manhattan mornings. Once a slightly antiquated piece of New York history, the building, with its recent renovations, was now the popular and quite public home of the Fantastic Four. The rooftop balcony, a part of the extensive space used as a home and office for Dr. Reed Richards, now carried the logo of the new group, the blazing and distinctive number four being the building's most recent acquisition.

Johnny Storm always felt an extra jolt of adrenaline when he saw the number sitting proudly in the sky. The dazzling, stylized number four was a symbol of his hard work, and the work of the best marketing agencies in the city. It was no secret that Johnny, initially, was no fan of the aging Baxter Building. When he first came here, in the time following their trip to space and their encounter with the cosmic storm, he thought the place was cramped and aging, two things he could hardly tolerate. Johnny was a fan of the new and the flashy—cars, watches, nightclubs, not to mention his notorious passion for new company, always female. But now that the building had been updated—Reed's laboratory expanded, proper offices for everyone in the group installed, the rooftop balcony with its stunning views of the city remodeled in time for the upcoming wedding—Johnny realized that this place was beginning to feel more like home. Besides, the Baxter Building was home to his favorite piece of real estate in all of Manhattan: the Fantastic Four Gift Shop.

Johnny walked quickly toward the entrance, blazing up the street in the early-morning rush. He liked to be there when the shop first opened, to make sure his standards were being met by the eager staff. If Reed had his laboratory upstairs, then Johnny considered the lobby store *his* lab—a place where his gifts could shine for the benefit of the world. And, more important, for the benefit of the Human Torch.

Johnny made his way under the Baxter Building's sign, with its elongated gold art-deco letters, through the glass revolving doors that had been replaced several times, since they always seemed to be the first things to get blown out or crushed. He greeted the morning staff in the lobby before stopping to see his work in all its glory. What used to be a dingy kiosk that sold tabloid magazines, salty snacks, and flat sodas was now a clean and crisp store filled with items bearing the logo of the Fantastic Four. Johnny's eyes lit up at the sight of the shirts, mugs, glasses, beach towels, and anything else he could think of filling the shelves of the shop. With the wedding fever that had come over Manhattan thanks to his sister's upcoming nuptials, he should have ordered more of the bridal veils and cummerbunds, all adorned with the group's logo. *Someone* had to feed the media frenzy, and he was more than happy to do it, if only to retain some control over how his team was portrayed and marketed. His sister often criticized him for this part of his job, but he knew she didn't quite understand that it was his way of protecting what they had, a way to keep the group together and fund Reed's many experiments. It wasn't so long ago that this building had held many mortgages and Reed had been sinking in debt. Johnny wanted to make sure that would never happen again. And if getting rich and famous was a by-product of his concern, so be it.

He walked into the clean, well-lighted space and made a beeline to his favorite thing: the Fantastic Four action figures. After running a finger across the shelves to check for dust, he started rearranging the items in the store to suit his critical retail eye, because something didn't sit right with him. He ignored the early-morning shoppers gawking at him and stopped a young female employee, her hair long and blond and almost reaching the Fantastic Four logo on her tight T-shirt.

Johnny stared into her blue eyes, trying to use his charm on her. *Employee motivation is important*, he thought, shifting the garment bag in his hand over his shoulder. "Okay, I've told you guys before," he said, motioning to the rows of action figures depicting the likenesses of Ben, his sister, Reed, and himself. "The Human Torches go in front because they're our biggest sellers." He gave her a big smile as the growing crowd in the gift shop hovered around them, obviously eavesdropping.

The female employee looked around sheepishly, twirling a long lock of hair around her finger. She chewed her gum slowly, staring intently at him. She tried to lower her voice to barely above a whisper. "Actually," she said, her cheeks reddening, "the *Thing* figure's been outselling all the others put together."

Johnny's face was still and unmoving as he tried to hide his surprise. He stared at the shelf of figures and saw a dozen Ben Grimms staring back at him. "I don't think so," he finally said, and continued moving the few Human Torch figures to the front. There seemed to be one of him for every five of Ben. Feeling out-numbered, he finally gave up. He gave the employee a quick smile, but not before putting his fist into the box of a Ben Grimm. He quickly made his way toward the elevators in the back of the lobby.

Upstairs, on the top floor of the building, Reed Richards was already hard at work. The center of the room held a large, circular laboratory, with equipment fanned out from its center. A mezzanine encircled the entire room from above. Living quarters led off from the mezzanine and housed the group. The most strik-ing aspect of the space was the row of floor-to-ceiling windows that led out to a rooftop deck, which offered some of the best views of Manhattan. It was Reed's fa-vorite part of the building, outside of his lab of course, and he usually took breaks by walking outside and ad-miring the skyline. It seemed fitting to him that this was where he would finally marry the love of his life, Susan Storm.

Reed sat inside the lab, near his main workstation. In the corner of the spacious room, a large object stayed hidden under a wide plastic tarp. The smooth

lines of the object were apparent through the clinging plastic, and part of a large pedestal could be seen
peeking out from underneath. Reed remained oblivious to it even though it took up a good amount of the
floor space in the lab. Instead, his focus lay on the work
directly in front of him. Reed had been reading with
great interest about the strange developments all over
the world: shock waves that appeared out of nowhere,
forests that spontaneously combusted, lakes and rivers
that inexplicably turned to rock and stone. Just the
other day, reports had come in from Giza that it was
snowing in the desert. He—like many others across
the globe—had seen the pictures of the Sphinx and
Pyramids covered in snow. He kept his investigations
secret so as not to worry Susan or the others, but each
new occurrence caused Reed to become more worried.
He typed data furiously into his PDA, a device that had
become even more helpful since Reed had souped it up
with an enhancement or five. His alterations made the
device look futuristic, yet still practical. The elaborate
keyboard helped Reed with his numerous calculations
and theorems, while its enhanced wireless capabilities
allowed him to hack into almost any computer system
on the planet.

Reed was lost in typing and thinking when Susan
walked into the main room from her office, just off the
center of the large, circular lab.

*   *   *

She was becoming increasingly frazzled with the combination of her normal workload and the task of almost single-handedly planning the wedding for the fifth time. She was an overachiever by nature—she had certainly proved that during her years at MIT—but enough was enough. She was feeling the frenzy of a soon-to-be bride through every inch of her body. She walked in to find Reed once again typing on his PDA, and she couldn't help but feel a bit annoyed.

She cleared her throat, a signal for her fiancé to stop typing. In a weary voice she said, "The city's charging us for three squad cars they say we destroyed." She held a wrinkled invoice in her hand, waving it in the air.

Reed, not picking up on her irritation, kept typing. "Uh-huh," he said distractedly.

She raised her voice. "It was during that armored-car robbery. I only remember *two* squad cars getting thrown." She let out a sigh. Why was she the only one who worried about these things?

"Sounds good."

The room fell silent, so Sue let out another long sigh.

Reed continued typing, oblivious to the growing annoyance of his fiancée.

Louder, she said, "Reed, are you listening to me?" Her eyes narrowed as she focused on Reed's PDA. She had begun to hate that damn device, even if Reed's modifications to it (she had to admit) were quite brilliant. It simply gave him another reason, another quite efficient and mobile reason, to be distracted. She focused her energy on the small device, summoning up the last threads of her focus. She had been practicing using her power and was becoming increasingly skilled at targeting her invisibility toward objects other than her own body. In a few seconds, she was able to turn the PDA in Reed's hand invisible.

Reed watched the device disappear from his sight, even if he could still feel the weight of it in his hand. "Right," he said quickly. "Putting it away." He swiveled in his chair and turned his full attention to her. "You were saying?"

Susan felt exasperated but grew less so under the weight of his gaze. He could always do that to her, once she got his attention. Her voice became softer as she began to speak. "A fitting in a half-hour. The musicians after that. There's just not enough time." Her shoulders fell with the admission. She suddenly felt very tired.

Reed stood up and walked over to her side. "Don't worry," he said consolingly. "Between the two of us, we'll get it all done." He offered her a smile, and then stretched it out across his entire face.

She smiled skeptically. "Really?" she asked. "And what were *you* just doing when I walked in? Writing your vows?"

Reed started to stammer, as he usually did when she

busted him. "I was just inputting my to-do list." He smiled at his recovery and took her hand. "Believe me, this wedding is the most important thing in my life."

Susan looked unconvinced.

"I promise," he said, and leaned in to kiss her. They were interrupted once again by the loud entrance of her brother.

Johnny stormed into the lab like a house on fire, ignoring the beautiful morning views of Manhattan and going directly to Reed and Susan. He carried with him a garment bag and held it up approvingly. "Hey, the new uniforms came in." He unzipped the bag and pulled one out. "What do you think?" he asked, holding it up for both to see.

Reed and Susan looked over to see their familiar blue suits, the ones Victor Von Doom had originally developed for their first trip together into space, riddled with company logos and labels. The special blue fabric was now a patchwork quilt of sponsorships from computer companies, food conglomerates, and automotive stores. Johnny had gotten the idea one weekend while watching NASCAR racers and was extremely pleased with the outcome. He looked eagerly at his sister to gauge her reaction. She remained silent, staring with wide eyes at the outfit. "What do you think?" he repeated.

Sue shook her head slowly, her jaw dropping slightly. She entertained the idea of turning the hideous uniform invisible but then decided not to. "I think there's no way I'm wearing that." Disgusted, she headed back to her office.

"What do you have against capitalism?" Johnny yelled after her, but she kept walking away, both hands covering her ears.

Reed decided not to comment on the ridiculous outfits and, once Susan had left the room, immediately turned back to his PDA, once again visible. He brought up the data about the recent strange events. The screen flashed as it reviewed the data marked ANOMALY ANALYSIS. Johnny, sensing he'd lost the attention of the crowd, dropped the uniform and garment bag and suddenly noticed the large tarp in the corner of the room. He stared at the strange shape covered in plastic. It appeared to be floating. "What's this?" he asked.

Reed kept typing into his PDA and responded, "Just a little hobby of mine."

Johnny started to walk closer to the hidden object. "Would it make a good toy or is it something . . . you know . . . *science-y*?"

Reed looked up briefly. He thought for a moment and then replied, "A little of both." He turned back to his device, obviously trying to input some new data. He held his thumbs over the enhanced device's keypad. He focused for a moment, then he split his thumbs into three separate miniature thumbs, each exactly alike, all of which started typing very quickly.

Johnny watched Reed and made a face. "I've always been both impressed and freaked out by that."

A smile broke over Reed's face. "Sue says I'm addicted to it," he said. He furrowed his brow in concentration and continued typing at a rapid speed, the miniature thumbs whizzing over the keyboard.

Johnny, watching the strange display, rolled his eyes. "I wonder why she'd say that."

Reed finished inputting the new data and pulled his fingers back together. He looked thoughtfully at the device, rubbing his chin. He turned to Johnny and in a conspiratorial voice said, "Keep it quiet, but I've cross-referenced and analyzed the global disturbances." He looked at Johnny to make sure he knew about the events he referred to. He was greeted by nothing but a blank stare but, knowing Johnny, that didn't mean anything. Reed paused for a moment before continuing. "They're being caused by cosmic radiation, not unlike the kind that gave us our powers."

Reed waited for the idea to register on Johnny's face, but he saw no reaction. Finally, Johnny began to speak. "Wow," he said, pausing for dramatic effect. "That's . . . really boring." Reed began to protest but Johnny stopped him. "Besides, I've got an important wedding issue to discuss with you."

Reed was taken aback by Johnny's sudden interest in the upcoming ceremony. Even though news of it had been plastered on television and in the newspapers, Johnny had kept a minimum safe distance from all aspects of planning the event. *If Sue is as overwhelmed as she seems to be,* Reed thought, *perhaps Johnny might be of some use.*

"Of course," Reed said, putting his PDA down. "What?"

Johnny smiled his widest grin and crossed his arms in front of his chest. "Your bachelor party."

Reed rolled his eyes. "No! Seriously, Johnny . . ."

Johnny put his hand out to interrupt Reed. "*John.* The focus testing showed that 'Johnny' skewed a little young."

Reed was becoming annoyed at the young man's prattling. He had too many things to do to listen to this. *Best to nip it in the bud,* he thought. "Seriously, Johnny." "No bachelor party. It's just not my kind of thing."

But Johnny would not be deterred. He knew Reed's number-one weakness, outside of Sue of course, was his best friend. "Then do it for Ben," he said, making his voice sound as sincere as possible. "This party means a lot to the big guy." He paused to let the suggestion work its way into Reed's head. "You're going to break his heart. He does have some kind of rock heart, doesn't he?"

Reed started to shake his head. "I've got too much to do before the wedding. And frankly, I think Sue might have a problem with it."

But Johnny wasn't about to back down. "You know what I think she'd have a problem with?" he asked, lowering his voice to sound threatening. "If someone told her you were actually investigating 'global disturbances' and 'cosmic radiation' instead of thinking only about the wedding, like you promised."

Reed gave in to the inevitable. "A bachelor party could be fun," he said reluctantly, putting away his PDA.

"*Yes!*" Johnny said, clapping his hands together.

"But," Reed countered, staring Johnny right in the eye, "no exotic dancers."

Johnny looked crestfallen, if only for a moment. "You disappoint me, Reed," he said, shaking his head. "You really do. But okay. You're going to have a blast tonight. Trust me." Johnny grabbed his hand and shook it intensely. Reed let his arm go slack and soon Johnny was shaking something with the consistency of wet pasta. He made a face and dropped the hand; it fell limply to the floor, along with the rest of Reed's outstretched arm.

Pulling his arm back to its natural shape, Reed realized that he was already having second thoughts, before Johnny even reached the elevator.

*   *   *

Ben Grimm, like many others in the city of Manhattan, was caught up in wedding fever. Even more so, since it was happening between two of his best friends. He'd known Reed and Sue were the perfect match since back in their days at MIT. It had taken a lot of wrestling and wrangling to get them both to this day, and Ben was going to make sure nothing was going to get in their way. Why else would he be putting himself through this?

He looked around the small tuxedo shop. Ben immediately felt claustrophobic when he walked in the joint, and the prolonged visit wasn't helping things. He had already snapped at Alicia twice. He couldn't help himself. Perhaps it was too much time spent in front of a mirror.

Ben felt Alicia's touch on his arm. Strange how just one touch from her could calm his rocky insides. Ever since he'd first met her in a Brooklyn bar, she'd had that effect on him. He admired the fact that her blindness didn't hold her back from doing the things she wanted to do. He took strength from that, too. *Imagine that*, he thought, staring at her slight shoulders and thin frame, *a little thing like that teaching this big monster new tricks*.

The tailor brought out the black tuxedo jacket. With his newfound celebrity, Ben had been surprised at how many companies had stepped forward to manufacture custom-made items to go with his new size.

Tennis shoes, clothing, even some electronic equipment. At times it was a relief, but other times it didn't seem to help at all. Nothing could change what he was. Not ever.

The tailor approached Ben hesitantly. Even with the advance notice, the man had trouble coming up with something that would fit Ben's wide, rocky frame. The man expertly slid on the oversized jacket, nimbly leading the soft fabric over Ben's arms and shoulders. He could feel Alicia's hand sliding up the fine fabric. *It's only a suit*, he told himself. *It's no big deal.*

Ben fidgeted in the jacket, trying to move his arms. "Feels a little snug," he said, almost apologetically, trying not to notice the tailor's impatient face. He tried to raise his hand and was met with a loud tearing noise. The jacket ripped almost in half, straight down the back.

"That didn't sound good," Alicia said, quickly bringing her hand to his forearm and letting it rest there. She knew how frustrated he could get. She couldn't see it, but she could feel it.

The tailor spoke up quickly, trying to placate Ben. "Don't worry. I'll let it out a few inches," he said, taking the ruined fabric off of Ben's frame. "Or a few feet," he muttered under his breath.

Ben turned to Alicia and saw her beautiful, unfocused eyes, staring in his direction. She couldn't see anything but still knew exactly what was going on. "Maybe I should just wear a muumuu," he said gruffly.

Alicia fumbled to find his large hand. She squeezed it as tightly as she could, even if Ben felt only a slight tingle. "You're going to be the handsomest man there. And I'm going to be the luckiest girl." She said the words softly, reaching up to stroke his cheek. She decided to change the subject. "Have you thought any more about me moving in?"

Ben pulled away quickly. "That's a big step, sweetie."

She had heard this from him before. They'd discussed living together many times. For all the reasons Ben could offer, she couldn't help but think it was something else. "You don't have to be afraid of it."

"Afraid? I'm not afraid. I just don't want to mess things up between us." As many times as he had said it, she just didn't understand. "What's the rush?" he asked again. "Things are going good the way they are."

Her only response, as always, was, "They could be *better*."

Ben was saved by the bell as the cell phone in his pocket began to ring. The high-pitched ring tone meant it was one of the Four calling. "I'd better get that," he said. He reached for his phone, an oversized custom-made model with large buttons, not totally dissimilar from those made for the elderly. It had been a gift from an aggressive communications company.

"What's up?" he answered gruffly. Alicia could hear his voice immediately soften. Then he said, "We're on our way." He took Alicia's hand as gently as he could. "Sue needs us."

They left the tailor's shop and rushed across town as quickly as they could. Ben couldn't really fit into a taxi, so that left them to navigate the busy streets of Manhattan on foot. Most of the crowd would part willingly when they saw Ben coming, out of either respect or fear. Alicia could only let him lead, at times holding on for dear life, as he weaved them through the crowd.

Ben stopped suddenly in front of a store with delicate white fabric covering the windows. Alicia could hear the whirring and clicking of cameras, along with the gruff voices of the photographers. Ben struck an impatient tone, and they plowed their way through the crowd of paparazzi trying desperately to look into the store windows.

The inside of the store was a marked contrast to the frenzy outside. Gentle classical music wafted through the store and its clean, uncluttered interiors gave Ben an instant feeling of calm. He ushered Alicia into the store, making eye contact with a security guard at the front door who looked relieved to have some backup.

Alicia could hear the soft music and smell the subtle hint of lavender in the air. The excited, hushed voices of the employees told her everything she needed to know. Ben led her through the front of the store to a secluded back room.

From behind a large white curtain they could both hear Sue's voice. "Okay, you guys ready?" A rustle of the curtain being pulled back and then, again, her voice. "Ta-da."

Ben stood there transfixed. He couldn't help it. He let out a loud gasp.

"That's the good kind of gasp, right?" Sue asked nervously.

Ben couldn't speak. He almost couldn't find the words. Finally he said, "You look gorgeous, Suzie." Alicia could hear the emotion in his voice.

His reaction got Sue excited, and she stared talking quickly. "Wait. I want you to see another one." She turned to go back into the dressing room, but Ben stopped her.

"Suzie, that's the one," he said.

Alicia moved forward tentatively, her hand out before her. Sue took her hand and led it to the full part of the dress. Alicia smiled as she ran her fingers along the lush, delicate fabric. "It's perfect," she whispered.

A lump formed in Sue's throat. She looked at Ben standing there, unable to take his eyes from her. She saw Alicia, so deftly and delicately touching the fabric of the dress, as if it were speaking to her. Something about the moment touched her deeply, and she could hardly keep from crying. Ben was right. This was the dress.

"This *is exactly* why I brought you guys," she said, wiping a tear from her cheek.

Half an hour later, they were ready to leave the bridal shop. Outside, the crowd of photographers was even more aggressive in trying to get a shot of Sue, especially now that her teammates were showing up. They smelled a scoop, not to mention the possibility of a photo of the bride-to-be in her gown for what the media dubbed "The Most Fantastic Wedding of All Time."

Ben opted to stay inside until the paparazzi thinned out a little before making his getaway, while Alicia and Sue stepped gingerly in front of the crowd. Sue was immediately assaulted by flashbulbs and lights. She noticed a group of regular people mixed in with the paparazzi, holding out sheets of paper and pens. With Alicia holding on to her arm, Sue tried to sign as many autographs as she could before the crush of people started to get to them. Sue felt like she couldn't breathe. She held up a hand, asking for some space.

"Okay," she said as calmly as she could. "We have to go now, guys. Thank you!"

She led Alicia away from the throngs of people, but they continued to be followed by one particularly aggressive photographer. Sue noticed him out of the corner of her eye. "Oh, it's this guy again. He is *so* annoying," she said loudly to Alicia. But he wasn't taking the hint. He continued to follow them closely, the clicking of his camera becoming faster and louder. He shoved the camera out in front of them, almost knocking Alicia down. Sue quickly focused and put up a small shield around her friend, pushing the photographer back a few steps.

Sue turned on her heel to face the man. "Can we have a little privacy, please?"

The photographer continued taking photos. "If you wanted privacy, you should have stayed home," he said from behind his camera, clearly trying to provoke an outburst from her. Johnny's often repeated refrain once again jumped into her head: *Photos of outbursts sell more newspapers. So don't do it.*

Sue didn't take the bait. "Of course. You're right," she said with a smile.

She grabbed Alicia and moved away. The photographer once again followed closely. He moved to the side to try to get in front of them. Suddenly, he slammed into the thin air and crumpled painfully to ground. A dark green lamppost slowly became visible again.

Alicia heard the sound of the man hitting the lamppost and the resounding *ping* of the metal. "Did you—?" she asked.

"Just keep walking," Sue said quickly, putting her arm around her friend. Her thoughts stirred rapidly. She had her dress. Everything was almost set. Nothing was going to stop this wedding from going forward. Nothing in this world.

3

SUE STORM SAT IN HER OFFICE, STARING OUT AT THE night. The surrounding lights of the Manhattan skyscrapers dappled her view. It had a calming effect on her, as did the fact that she finally had some time alone. Their entire floor at the Baxter Building was blissfully deserted. Her brother had taken Reed and Ben out for the evening. *Boys only*, he had said, and although Sue feared the trouble those three might get into, at the moment she was just too relaxed to care. Besides, the thought of them out together brought a huge smile to her face. She knew the men of the group needed some downtime, just as she did.

She walked out onto the rooftop deck, savoring the view of the city. The moon was thin, a perfect crescent. The wind was brisk and cool. The city was almost quiet. She absolutely loved Manhattan on nights like these. She breathed the air in deeply and made her way back inside. *Yes*, she thought, *it feels good to spend some time alone*.

Down on the street, a large black suburban with government plates screeched to a halt in front of the

Baxter Building. The doors were pushed open quickly, and several soldiers leapt out of the imposing car. One figure led the rest—a grizzled man with a creased face and a dour expression. His skin was as dark as the night, his hair closely cropped to his head. General George Hager had served his country for his entire adult life and disliked New York City—a town of liberal hippies and communists, as he was often quoted as saying—as much as he disliked the building he was about to enter. He scoffed as they made their way into the lobby and past the Fantastic Four Gift Shop. He exchanged a look of disgust with his aide, Captain Raye, an attractive woman with ice-blue eyes, sharp angular cheekbones, and an equally dour demeanor. She walked quickly, not unlike a model on a runway, but with a much more serious task at hand.

The figures piled quickly into the gilded elevators of the Baxter Building and Hager pushed the button for the top floor. They walked out of the elevator and into the reception area. Hager and Raye came to a sudden halt when they saw a receptionist standing behind a desk. They had assumed that the staff would have already gone home for the evening. The receptionist was tall and plain, her hair pulled back in a sensible bun, a smile painted on her thin face. Her vision was focused on nothing in particular, and her facial expression didn't change with the arrival of a group of military men. Her voice, when she spoke, had a strange mechanical feel to it: "Ms. Storm will be with you shortly." Something about her eyes and voice made General Hager suspicious. He put his arm out and swept it right through her body. The image of the receptionist shimmered, revealing her to be nothing more than a hologram. Raye let out a small gasp just as Sue walked into the lobby.

"Thanks, Rebecca," Sue said politely to the hologram. It suddenly shut itself down and the receptionist faded into thin air. Sue didn't try very hard to mask the annoyance in her voice as she turned to Hager. "Can I help you?"

Hager took in a deep breath. "We're here to see Dr. Richards."

"I'm sorry," she said slowly. "He's not in right now. Is there anything I can do for you?" Her polite smile did not match the chilly tone of her voice.

Hager met her tepid smile with his steely gaze. "Yes," he said, "you can take us to see Dr. Richards."

The Invisible Woman sighed. "O-*kay*. I guess my quiet, solitary evening had to end eventually. Come with me, General."

Across town, a line of people stood waiting in the cold night to enter the newest and trendiest nightclub in all of Manhattan. Ambient noise from behind the double steel doors excited those waiting to get in as a mixture of heat and deep bass could be felt coming from inside. The highly polished doors gave those waiting something to do as they checked their reflections, their skin, at least briefly, colored a light shade of silver.

Johnny led his reluctant, aging troops into the main room of the club. He'd fought tough battles before, but nothing like this. *Why is it so hard to get these two to loosen up?* he thought as he pushed them into the heart of the nightclub. The large space was filled almost to capacity with gorgeous girls and well-groomed men. In the center of the rectangular room was a dance floor made of metal, and its silver sheen made the lights dance and reflect that much more rapidly. Ben looked uncomfortable. Reed looked confused. Johnny felt great.

"This is it?" Ben asked. Johnny nodded enthusiastically, pointing to a tiny banner on a faraway wall, barely visible in the shifting light of the club, that read, CONGRATULATIONS, REED.

Reed put his fingers in his ears, trying to hear himself think over the roar of the crowd. "I don't know anyone here," he said, a bit flummoxed.

Johnny dismissed the comment as if swatting away a fly. "Yeah, I would have invited your friends, but you don't really have any."

Reed was getting even more confused. "What about the Nobel committee?" Johnny let out a laugh, and even Ben rolled his eyes at that one.

Johnny explained himself. "Sorry, I mean you don't really have any friends that I want to party with." He swept his hands out to the dance floor, eyebrows raised, as if offering the crowed room as an alternative.

On cue, a trio of screaming girls in small, tight dresses came over to them. Johnny's eyes traveled all over a blonde in a silver metallic dress. He started to make his move.

Reed reached out his hand and stopped him. "Johnny, we had a deal."

Johnny put his hands out in front of him, making a gesture of innocence. "Hey, they're not exotic dancers, all right?" His eyes once again burned all over the beautiful women. "They're just *hot*," he yelled and grabbed the blonde, leading her to the dance floor. The other girls swarmed Reed, running their fingers through the gray hair around his temples and grabbing his shoulders.

"You're Mr. Fantastic, aren't you?" one of the girls asked. "That is so awesome!" She lead Reed away from the bar and toward the dance floor.

Ben, standing alone, turned to the bartender. He ignored the surprised look on the guy's rugged face. "I need a pitcher of beer with the biggest handle you got," Ben said.

About an hour later, the club was in full swing. The line in front stretched around the block, leaving the silver-hued would-be patrons shivering in the cold evening. Reed's banner had quickly and mysteriously been burned to ash. At the bar, Johnny and his new friends lined up a row of sambuca shots. He turned his finger to flame and ignited the shots. The crowd around them applauded as they tossed the drinks back. Even Ben smiled before downing a pitcher of beer in one gulp. He slammed the pitcher down on the granite bar, cracking the counter. A long, low belch followed.

Reed, too, was beginning to enjoy himself. The music, after a while, was infectious, as was the rambunctious dancing of the lithe bodies on the floor. He was even growing used to the rapt attention of the two girls he'd met when they first arrived at the club. They hung on his every word, enjoying the free drinks that Johnny kept sending over. The two girls didn't have much to say, but that was fine by him. Reed was more than happy to do the talking for all of them.

"When the universe began," he said, not noticing one of the girls stifling a yawn, "it was no bigger than a marble. Then, BANG!" He raised his voice and expanded his hands for dramatic effect. The girls squealed and jumped at the unexpected use of his power, his limbs stretching out a few feet in either direction. He smiled at them both and continued. "It exploded, and in a trillionth of a second it expanded exponentially into what became the universe we know today." He pulled his arms back in and took a long pull from his very strong drink.

"Wow," said one of the girls, named Sandy. "You're really *smart*."

"Thank you, Candy. That means a lot to me." Reed's voice was getting a little hoarse from his trying to talk over the loud dance music, but it wouldn't let up. As one song ended, another one began immediately.

"I love this song," exclaimed the other girl, Amy or Amber. Reed couldn't remember. "You want to dance?"

Reed put up his hands in a show of mock defeat. "No, I don't really."

The girl in the metallic silver dress joined in, leaving Johnny to cool his jets at the bar with Ben. "Come on!" she yelled, walking past them.

The girls quickly pulled Reed out onto the dance floor. The reflective metal floor added to his general disorientation as the bodies around him moved to a beat he couldn't quite seem to find. At the bar, Johnny poked Ben in the ribs, bruising his elbow. They watched, amused, as Reed tried to keep up with the three girls moving around him.

"Just loosen up. Have some fun," Sandy told him, moving her arms in the air. Reed started to let the music wash over him, the guiding hands of the girls helping him find a rhythm in the loud electronic music. He began to relax, feeling his body getting loose. The girls started to clap and encouraged him as Reed became more daring with his moves, his body being led by the pulsing beats and deep bass of the music. His mind and focus slipped as his body lost its shape, his arms stretching and flying out into the air. His legs stretched, propelling his body upward without his feet leaving the metal dance floor. His arms were like ribbons come alive, bending and twisting around the large room. For once, Reed detached his body from his mind and gave himself over to the music.

At the bar, Ben and Johnny stood with their jaws dropped. Neither could remember ever seeing Reed like this. Johnny, dodging a flying hand and a bit envious of the attention, said to Ben, "When he loosens up, he *really* loosens up."

Across the crowded club, near its main entrance, a gaggle of onlookers watched in rapt attention as Reed added his powers to the thrumming beat of the music. Just behind them, Ben saw Sue and a bunch of military brass enter the room, followed by the hulking figures of club security. Ben recognized General Hager and knew that his presence meant trouble.

"Where is he?" Hager asked.

Sue pointed to her fiancé on the dance floor, who was suddenly doing the wave with his long, outstretched arms. "There," she said to Hager. "Unfortunately. For him."

Reed spotted Sue and her stone-faced entourage. With reddening cheeks, he pulled his body back into shape, oblivious to the drinks his waving arms knocked over at different tables around the club. He readjusted his coat once his arms snapped back, then rushed over to greet his fiancée. Ben lumbered over to join them, the crowd parting for him.

"Sue! Hi!" Reed said. He looked over at the man with the ramrod posture standing next to her. "General Hager?"

Hager made no attempt to hide his contempt. "Can we speak somewhere private?"

Sue crossed her arms and raised an eyebrow. "Unless you need to do some Jell-O shots off someone's stomach." Ben snickered at the comment. Hager grunted and motioned toward the back of the club.

They left the main room of the club and entered the kitchen, a spare, clean space also outfitted with silver metal. Noticing the look on Hager's face, as well as the military escort, the staff cleared out quickly. Reed led Hager to the back of the kitchen, away from the stoves and oven. The military escort kept close to the general, followed by Ben, Sue, and a now intrigued Johnny, who kept trying to catch the eye of Hager's attractive aide. Sue leaned in to Ben and asked in a whisper, "How does Reed know the general?"

Ben whispered, "A few years back, the guy was trying to push a new missile defense system. Reed testified the technology wouldn't work. The general wasn't too happy about it." The whispering stopped as the general began to speak.

"I'm only here, Richards, because I'm under direct orders from the Joint Chiefs of Staff. Personally, I don't like the idea of sharing sensitive information with a civilian scientist—especially one who loves the public spotlight so much." The general threw a hard look at both Reed and Johnny.

Reed spoke up. "Always a pleasure to see you, too, General. What can I do for you?"

Hager ignored Reed's tone and continued. "As you may know, there have been recent, unusual occurrences all over the world. Officially, we've downplayed their significance to the public. But we're concerned these anomalies might pose a credible threat to our national security."

The grizzled general turned to his aide and nodded. She pulled a file out of a metal briefcase and handed the file over to Reed. "This was taken by one of our spy satellites three days ago," she explained to him.

Reed opened the file, marked CONFIDENTIAL, and pulled out a grainy satellite photograph. The picture showed a silvery blur just above the Earth, followed by a wake of radiant energy. Ben and the others peered over Reed's shoulder to see the photo.

"What is it?" Ben asked.

"We have no idea," Hager replied, nodding in

Reed's direction. "We were hoping Dr. Richards here could tell us."

"I'm afraid I have never seen anything like it," Reed responded. "Ben?"

Ben Grimm stared at the photograph, searching his vast knowledge to try to come up with some kind of explanation. "I'd say it was a meteor or a piece of space junk burning up in the atmosphere, but the trail's all wrong." He paused to consider his words. "This thing's giving off some kind of energy."

General Hager's face showed his concern. "Take a look at this," he said. "Captain Raye." The aide brought up an image on a laptop computer. It showed huge craters in the most isolated locations on the planet: the Amazon rain forest, the Australian outback, the Ural Mountains. All of the craters were uniform in size and equally round, perfectly smooth, their walls made of a reflective silver metal.

Captain Raye said, "They've been appearing in remote areas all over the world since the events started."

"Have you identified the silver alloy?" Reed asked her.

She shook her head. "It's not any known element."

Hager spoke up quickly. "If we're going to find out what this is all about, we need a way to locate and intercept that object."

Reed's mind already appeared to be wandering, examining the mysterious object and the problems it presented from a variety of directions. He said, "It would be possible to build a sensor, tie it into the Baxter Building's satellite grid, then pinpoint the exact location of the object."

A small look of relief crossed Hager's face. "Good. So you'll build it for us."

Reed started to nod his head in agreement but stopped himself. He looked at Sue's face, which was filled with both concern and curiosity about these anomalies.

"I'm afraid I can't," he said.

Hager's tone was unmistakable. His relief had turned back to contempt. "What?"

The group exchanged puzzled looks, while Johnny once again tried to make eye contact with Captain Raye. She held her focus on the general.

Reed cleared his throat and spoke up. "General, I'm getting married this Saturday. So I just don't have the time." He locked eyes with Sue, who gave him her sweetest smile.

Hager was outraged. "Richards, your country needs your help."

Reed pulled out a business card and scribbled a number just under the name. "Call this man—Professor Jeff Wagner. He's head of the physics department at Brown. I am sure he can help."

The tone of the general's voice made Reed uneasy.

Hager wasn't used to not getting his way, and he had no problem showing it. "I expected more. Even from you." The temperature of the room fell by degrees and Reed doubted that even Johnny could heat up the chill caused by the general. General Hager turned on his heel, Captain Raye right behind him. He led his entourage out of the kitchen. They plowed their way through the still crowded club and back onto the street, where they started to pile back into their big, imposing SUVs.

Johnny walked up to Captain Raye. "Hi," he said. "John Storm, Fantastic Four Incorporated. Have you ever done any professional modeling?" He gave her his best, most incendiary smile.

A curt "Not interested" was her only response.

Johnny was undeterred. " 'Cause you got the most amazing . . ."

"Not interested!" Captain Raye said again, forcefully and loud enough for the others to hear. She climbed quickly in to the passenger side of the black SUV and slammed the door shut.

Johnny was left standing on the curb. His voice hadn't lost a bit of its enthusiasm when he said, "Wow. A challenge. I like it."

Sue ignored her brother's shenanigans and turned to Reed. Her face had a tender look and the streetlights bathed her features in a soft glow. "I can't believe you just turned down a science project."

Reed took her hands in his. "They can build a sensor without me. The most important thing right now is our wedding. No interruptions. No postponements." He emphasized his words with small kisses on her hand.

"Okay," she said softly. She kissed him on the lips.

Reed pulled away. "And listen, about what you saw back at the bar—"

She laughed and interrupted him. "Reed, don't worry about it. I *know* you, okay? I'm glad you had fun."

"Thank you," he said, sounding relieved.

"Besides," she added quickly, "it was *nothing* compared to what I did at my bachelorette party. Talk about wild!"

She gave him a wide smile and walked away, leaving him standing on the curb. His questions—"Wild? How wild? Sue?"—echoed down the empty street.

Ben stood there silently, watching the team of SUVs disappear down the street. The satellite photo stuck eerily in his mind. He had a feeling deep in his gut that something was coming. Something bad. Something they had never encountered before.

4

THE LARGE FRAMED TAPESTRIES SEEMED TO BE SUS-pended from the walls of the mansion, floating in the dark and forgotten space. Each painting featured one solitary figure clad in armor and holding a weapon. History may have banished these figures to oblivion, but here the portraits were generous: taking away their blemishes and plagues, casting their cadaverous skin in hues of sunlight and shadow, turning their blood-stained weapons an attractive shade of crimson to offset the pale carpets and walls. The portraits por-trayed a line of warriors, the kind that used to rule this forgotten European village, back when gold and land meant wealth and power. In each portrait, a Von Doom held the family's faceplate, an ancient piece of metallic jewelry, forged in fire generations ago. To each of the figures in the paintings, the faceplate was worth more than gold, for it symbolized a power that could be passed down to each succeeding generation. Power was important, they knew, but power increased exponen-tially throughout history was limitless. Unstoppable. A dynasty.

Victor Von Doom had been spending a great deal of time in the hall of portraits. It helped him somehow, not being the only dead man in the mansion.

He ran his eyes over the portraits once again, the rich canvases framed in old wood newly polished to a shine by his own deformed hand. The men trapped in the paintings would be surprised to learn that their most recent scion had earned his wealth and power not through brute force and strength but through the more nimble manipulations of corporate business and advanced technologies. Von Doom Enterprises was once a billion-dollar company, a cutting-edge leader in many fields, and Victor's perfect face once adorned the cover of magazines the same way these portraits covered the walls. But that was before. Before Reed Richards reentered his life. Before the cosmic storm. He lost everything because of that man—his company, his life, and, most important, Susan. He'd been shucked back into this isolated tomb without so much as a thought. Victor wondered what his ancestors would say about that.

He stared at the portraits one more time. Perhaps it was time to return to his roots, back to the essence of his family's fortune and power: brute strength. No more disguises.

Victor left the hallway, running his hand over his scarred and burned face. He winced in pain as he touched it. He couldn't yet bring himself to stare too long in the mirror. He entered a large room secreted toward the back of the manse. Victor's new laboratory was protected by thick stone walls, and by the fact that everyone thought he was dead. Open storage crates sat haphazardly around the large room, revealing high-tech equipment. A bank of computers took up an entire wall. Assorted weaponry that could fund a small revolution (and many of the weapons had done just that) lay scattered across the floor and several tables. Two satellite dishes sat in one corner of the room, waiting to be added to the others already in service. Victor looked around at the cherished relics of his former life, his former company. These were the spoils of his last war, his most painful defeat. But he would use them to launch something new. Something that would allow Victor to emerge victorious.

A wide bank of flat LCD television monitors brought the modern world into the medieval mansion, reintroducing Victor to events occurring around the globe. He dismissed most of the frivolous news channels, with their features on politics or celebrity or upcoming weddings, and instead focused on the ones closer to home. He was silent as he watched the news from his homeland, this isolated strip of forgotten culture. He felt assaulted by images of starving people dressed in rags waiting in line for bread or water; clips of riots breaking out over the presence of a stray chicken or goose; miles and miles of wasted, empty roads, littered with the suffering and starving of his people. His ancestors would cringe if they could see what modernity had done to Latveria.

More than one video monitor had been thrown against the wall, a victim of his rage. But today, Victor called up the image he had become obsessed with: a satellite photograph of a silver object entering Earth's lower atmosphere. Written across the image were the words UNITED STATES SPY SATELLITE EPSILON, TRANSMISSION 89337 INTERCEPTED. Victor once again studied the photo, feeling deep within his gut that this object was a symbol. A catalyst for change. Redemption.

He held the image in his metal hand, whispering in a menacing voice, "What *are* you? More important, what can you do for *me*?"

The laboratory of Reed Richards was humming with activity. He'd risen at dawn, eager to speak with Professor Jeff Wagner about his unsettling and quite unexpected meeting with General Hager. Reed stared at the video console that showed him the face of the elderly academic, who looked like a cross between Albert Einstein and Woody Allen. Wagner was already complaining to Reed about the general's gruff demands.

"Reed," Wagner continued in a cracked voice, "I told the general it would take me months, maybe years, to figure out how to construct this kind of sensor."

Reed dismissed the professor's penchant for drama. "It's not that difficult," he said, thinking *This man needs to get out more often*.

"I'm doing everything I can," he said. "But we need your help on this. Maybe you could take a few minutes away from playing super hero to work on some real science." Leaving those words burning in Reed's ears, the professor angrily signed off.

Reed let out a deep sigh, already exhausted. He didn't understand the professor's inability to work on his own. *Science by committee*, he thought. *Figures*. Reed scrolled through his wedding to-do list, which didn't seem to be getting any shorter. The display screen on his PDA listed a host of various errands: pick up Sue's ring, arrange limousine transports, double-check flower arrangements (Sue was allergic to orchids), pick up the wedding cake. He tossed the PDA aside, glad to be rid of it. When had such a simple ceremony become so complicated? As eager as Reed was to have the event over with, he admitted to himself that the real source of his anxiety was not his upcoming nuptials. The true origin of his concern was a certain satellite photo of an unknown silver entity reaching Earth. That, and the accompanying strange disturbances and mysterious craters. They had to be related. Reed stared once again at the photo of the silver object. He knew he had to do something.

That night, Reed worked under the cover of a bright

moon laced with a silver glow. The rooftop deck, where he would soon marry Susan, was covered with equipment and tools and scraps of metal. Reed stretched himself thin all over the space, hastily building a large satellite antenna. Sweat appeared on his brow as he worked at a feverish pace, trying to finish his project under the cover of darkness.

The guts of the device were exposed, showing a mess of circuitry and wiring extending across the floor of the deck. Reed uploaded data into the antenna using his PDA, once again typing with multiple digits at a furious pace. *I can do this*, he thought to himself. *I can do it all: help Hager and Wagner and get married and no one will be the wiser. No one will know.*

Just as he finished the thought, Ben Grimm stepped out onto the deck, causing the entire roof to shudder slightly. The motion startled Reed, who looked up from his PDA quickly. He let out a sigh of relief at the sight of Ben.

"What are you doing up here?" Ben asked.

"Nothing," Reed said, trying to push a group of wires away with his foot. "Just needed some air."

Ben looked unconvinced. "You're building that thing for the general, aren't you?"

Reed nodded his head reluctantly. He should have known better than to try to pull one over on his best friend.

Ben surveyed the mess around the roof that in a few

days would house the wedding guests—all their friends and family. Sue would have a coronary if she saw what a mess Reed had made. "I'm guessing Sue doesn't know about this?" Ben asked. Reed motioned around the roof and gave him a look. Ben relented, putting his large hands up in the air, saying, "My lips are sealed. Or they would be, if I had 'em."

Reed was grateful but not surprised. He knew he could count on Ben. But then a new thought entered his mind. "And don't tell Johnny," Reed added.

Just then, a bright flame appeared in the sky. At first it looked like a low-flying shooting star as it headed directly for the roof of the building. But the familiar colors soon became visible: swirling flames of red and orange. Johnny landed on the rooftop deck and smothered his flames, but his ears were still burning.

"Don't tell Johnny what?" he asked.

How does he do that? Reed thought. But he said only "Great."

Johnny surveyed the mess of circuitry and wires all over the floor of the deck. His eyes ran up to the large piece of metal that was the main body of the sensor. "Hey—you're building that thing, aren't you? Man, when Sue finds out, you're going to get an invisible kick in the nuts."

Ben knew Johnny wasn't wrong. "We're keeping it quiet."

Johnny ignored Ben and turned to Reed. "I thought you had too much wedding stuff to do."

Once again, Johnny wasn't wrong. "Actually, that *is* a problem." Reed checked the list on his PDA again. Just looking at it made him feel hopeless. "I don't know how I'm going to get it all done."

Ben Grimm saw the look of concern on his best friend's face and decided to step up. "Don't worry," he said, corralling Johnny with a thick, rocky arm. "We'll help you out."

"We will?" Johnny asked, trying to free himself from Ben's grip. Ben nodded his head, glaring at the young hotshot.

The next few days Ben and Johnny ran themselves ragged, performing all the tasks Reed had promised to do. Traveling through the crowded streets of Manhattan, they saw firsthand how much the city was in the grip of wedding fever. They were followed constantly by paparazzi, who were trying to guess their every move. Worse, the photographers always seemed to be one step ahead of them. No detail was too small to be discovered, no errand too superfluous to warrant a herd of clicking cameras and flashing bulbs. As annoyed as Johnny was to have to do all of Reed's dirty work, the constant attention made it almost worth his while.

The next afternoon, Ben and Johnny managed to elude their pursuers and duck into a jeweler's shop in the diamond district, just north of Times Square. The jeweler, well known and selected by Reed for his discretion, ushered the two into a back room, where they could remain undisturbed. There, amid cases of glittering diamonds and other jewels, he carefully opened a large safe concealed behind a wall panel. He pulled out a small velvet box and opened it slowly for Johnny and Ben. They both stepped back a pace, as if he were holding a weapon. The jeweler couldn't help but laugh to himself at how awkward they both were over a piece—even such a *substantial* piece—of jewelry. He took the ring out of the box and tossed it to Ben. Surprised by the sudden action, Ben caught it too hard and watched as the ring was crushed in his rocky grip. The jeweler turned white.

"That's impossible!" he said, stumbling over the words as they tried to leave his mouth. "We have only the finest-quality jewelry, guaranteed to last for generations. This has never happened before." He thought he was going to faint.

Who's laughing now? Johnny thought. "That's because you never had to deal with the 'Two-Ton Kid,'" he said, patting his rocky shopping companion on the back. Security escorted them both to the door.

Later, Ben and Johnny were stuck in traffic going up Park Avenue, just north of Grand Central Station. Taxis honked incessantly at them, either to say hello or to complain about Ben's driving. His custom-made SUV wasn't much larger than the regular models, but in a city already cramped for space, it stuck out like a sore thumb. It also, unfortunately, made them an easy target for the photographers following them. As did Johnny, who was hanging out the passenger-side window, leaving a trail of fire over their car wherever they went.

Ben finally parked in front of their destination, an upscale bakery on the Upper East Side of Manhattan. They went into the store to pick up Reed's one-of-a-kind cake. The shopkeeper, a young woman who happened to be a big Human Torch fan, had also made up some cupcakes with the group's logo on them. A few polite bites later, Ben pushed Johnny out of the store, carrying a huge, frosted wedding cake in one of his large, platter-sized hands. Approaching his car, Ben could see that size once again worked to his disadvantage; his SUV was sandwiched between two other cars with barely an inch of space between them. Ben handed the cake to Johnny, who struggled under its weight and feared he might start to melt the frosting. Ben stepped out into the street and picked his car up, lifting it over his head and placing it gently back on the pavement, free of the closely parked cars.

While Ben was busy with his car, Johnny tried to keep an even footing under the weight of the multi-tiered cake. He kept his eyes on the top of it, where the plastic bride and groom were standing in rich butter-cream frosting. He heard the steady clicking of high heels on the pavement and turned to see a leggy redhead walking by, a tight Fantastic Four T-shirt stretching itself across her ample chest. His jaw dropped suddenly. So did the cake.

Ben stood there glaring at Johnny, whose hands were covered in melted frosting.

Their final stop was the florist, located in the flower district, just north of Greenwich Village. Johnny was ordered to wait out by the car while Ben went in to pick up Susan's order. He came out weighed down by dozens of baskets of centerpieces: bright flowers arranged with twigs, ferns, and other various greenery—and no orchids. Ben noticed the absence of photographers and breathed a sigh of relief. His focus turned to his full load as he navigated the cracked sidewalk to reach his SUV. Ben managed to get the entire forest of flowers into the back of the truck. Just then, a centerpiece fell out of the overloaded truck and onto the street. Johnny, not wanting to appear unhelpful, kneeled down and picked it up, then handed it to Ben.

A photographer appeared from behind a group of parked cars. He quickly snapped a photo, just as Ben was taking the flowers from Johnny. They exchanged a worried look.

Jeez, Johnny thought. *This wedding better be worth it.*

5

THE RISING SUN ON THE MORNING OF REED AND Susan's wedding was yet another spotlight to shine on the big event. Even the heavens seemed interested. The Baxter Building was crawling with security guards making sure only guests and appropriate personnel gained entrance. Ben and Johnny's hard work had paid off: the space looked perfectly suited for an elegant wedding. The rooftop deck was adorned with flowers in each of its four corners. White chairs fanned out from a long row of carpet leading toward the domed white pergola where the couple would exchange their vows. Flowers scaled the height of the pergola and dripped down on all sides in gentle, fragrant cascades. Beyond the wood structure sat the breathtaking view of the city. Tall skyscrapers buffeted the elegant rooftop deck, their silver facades reflecting the warm and bright sunlight. Overhead, helicopters buzzed like hungry mosquitoes, trying to film the event for the legion of fans out there hoping to get a glimpse of the fantastic bride.

Down on the street, traffic snarled for blocks as legitimate guests worked their way through the dozens of police cars and media vehicles already swarming the site. Cops stood watch on foot as well as on horseback, trying to keep the flow of guests moving and the avalanche of reporters at bay. The great city of New York was no stranger to this type of high-profile event, and the police had the same presence as would benefit a visiting world leader or president. But a wedding, especially one as public as this, was a different affair. Excitement filled the streets like it was New Year's Eve in Times Square.

Upstairs in his lab, groom-to-be Reed Richards tried to isolate himself from the frenzy down on the streets. Truth be told, it wasn't hard to do. Reed had been pushing himself for days, trying to get the sensor online for General Hager, and exhaustion showed on his usually elastic features. His eyes were thin and dry, his face a grizzled carpet of unshaved stubble.

Ben Grimm walked in to see the disheveled figure of his best friend. Dressed to the nines in a tuxedo that actually fit, Ben was a bit surprised to find Reed in such a state. Reed barely noticed Ben's entrance, focused instead on the final adjustments he was making to the sensor. A video monitor next to Reed showed the sensor antenna on the roof, not far from the main entrance of the wedding guests. Johnny had wanted to put some flowers over it, but Reed did not want anything to interfere with its signal.

Ben cleared his throat and spoke loudly. "Reed, come on! You're going to miss your own wedding."

Reed looked up to see his friend in formal wear. A smile crossed his face. "Almost done."

Reed turned back to the video monitor, which now showed the dour face of General Hager. "General, I'm putting the sensor online now." Reed punched a few buttons on the console and the machine hummed to life. "There. If there's a surge in cosmic radiation anywhere on the planet, you'll know about it."

"Let's hope so," the general barked. "We've already gotten reports of two more craters."

Two more? Reed thought, growing more concerned. He knew he better keep track of the general's progress. He pulled out his PDA. "Just linking it to my PDA . . . and that's it."

Ben's impatience was growing, even with the news of the appearance of two more craters. "Great. Now will you please shave and put on your tux? You're getting married in two hours and you look like a bum."

Reed set his PDA down on the table. "Absolutely." He started to walk toward his room but stopped suddenly. A look of anxiety crossed his face. "Oh my God! I'm getting married." Even for someone who could stretch his body to great lengths, Reed's knees appeared a little wobbly.

Ben was at his side, holding his friend up by his lab coat. "There we go," he said, leading Reed down the

74

hall to his quarters, one foot elongated and dragging behind them.

Susan Storm looked out the window of her dressing room at the crowds and traffic below. The butterflies in her stomach were turning into something much larger as anxiety flooded her body. *All this time planning,* she thought, *and now it's finally here. For the fifth time.* As much as she had imagined how this day would feel, she found herself continually looking outside. The police, the traffic, the helicopters. It wasn't the warm, intimate ceremony she had hoped for.

Behind her, Alicia felt for the clasp and zipped up Sue's floor-length white gown. Alicia's fingers were so nimble that Sue didn't feel a thing.

"This isn't how I imagined it," she confessed.

Alicia stepped in front of her, looking beautiful in her maid-of-honor gown. "Nothing ever is," she replied.

But Sue couldn't shake the bad feeling she'd woken up with that morning. "Alicia, this just doesn't feel right."

Alicia tried to comfort her friend. "It's okay. Even super heroes can have wedding-day jitters."

Sue felt her eyes welling with tears, the feeling in the pit of her stomach growing stronger. "It's more than that. Is my life always going to be a circus? Can we raise a child in . . . all *this?*" She banged her fist against the glass, her only recourse against the swarm of media outside the building. All those eyes peering at them with their cameras and flashbulbs and lights. "Face it, we're not exactly *normal*."

Alicia took Sue's hand, trying to calm her down. "Ben and I aren't exactly a 'normal' couple, either. But that doesn't stop us from being happy. Do you love Reed?"

A tear fell silently down Sue's cheek, and she said, "More than I've ever loved anyone."

Alicia squeezed Sue's hand to emphasize her point. "Then there's your answer."

The two women hugged. Sue felt comforted by the words of her good friend; Alicia was right. Sue had to believe that she and Reed, together, could rise above whatever obstacles might come their way, big or small.

Sue turned away from Alicia, catching a glimpse of her face in the mirror.

Oh no. It couldn't be. And of all days. It figured, with all the stress . . .

"Oh, *great*!" Sue exclaimed in frustration.

"What?" Alicia's voice was filled with concern.

Sue looked closer at her reflection, confirming her suspicions. "I've got a zit."

"Don't panic. We'll find some base—"

"No, it's okay." Sue looked in the mirror, concentrating intently on the blemish . . . concentrating . . .

until it completely disappeared. Turned invisible, actually. She breathed a sigh of relief, more for the fact that it was one less thing the media jackals could rabidly obsess over. For the moment, anyway.

"Crisis averted," Sue declared. "Now . . . all I have to do is concentrate on it continuously for the next eight hours."

Right in the middle of the crowd, where he usually liked to be, Johnny Storm was dodging police on horseback. He pulled up to the Baxter Building in his fire-red sports car and revved the powerful, expensive engine for the crowd before turning off the ignition. His date, a shapely young woman with hair that matched the car, sat beside him, obviously thrilled with the crowds.

"Look at these parasites," he said to her with a big grin on his chiseled face.

"Terrible," she said, adjusting her chest for the camera.

"Have they no shame whatsoever?" he asked in a mock-sincere voice. Johnny jumped out of the car, straightening his brand-new tuxedo jacket as the camera crews and reporters swarmed him. He raised his hand for silence. "Hey! Listen up! This is the most important day of my sister's life, so I just want to tell all of you . . . to check out our website, www.fantastic-four-inc.com, for all the latest news, merchandise, and fan-club information." The surrounding crowd started to roar and cheer. "Thank you!" Johnny yelled, holding his hands in the air. He took the hand of his voluptuous date and they made their way through the crowd toward the entrance of the Baxter Building. A reporter grabbed Johnny's arm, shoving a microphone in his face and asking, "What's it take to date the Human Torch?"

A grin spread like fire across his face. "Fireproof lingerie and a lot of aloe." His date winked to the camera before they disappeared through the revolving door.

They took the elevator up to Reed's lab. After depositing his date with the other guests on the roof, Johnny entered Reed's room to find Ben Grimm staring at his reflection in a mirror, adjusting his large bow tie.

"Hey, it's the Big Rock Candy Mountain!" he teased.

Ben grimaced at him. "You're late."

"Look," Johnny said, "let's not make today about *me*. It's Sue and Reed's special day. Let's give *them* the attention for a change." He adjusted his bow tie in the mirror next to Ben.

"Just keep it quiet," Ben warned. "I'm going over my toast in my head."

Johnny made a face. "I still don't know why Reed picked you to be best man instead of me. I mean, let's face it, you're not the best, and you're barely a man."

"You know," Ben said, turning to face him, "it'd be real easy to turn this wedding into a funeral. I already got the tux."

They were interrupted by a delicate knock on Reed's door. Alicia entered the room, fingering the wall. Ben looked at her in her beautiful gown and smiled. "Hey, sweetie."

"I got your boutonniere," she said, holding a large flower in her hand. She started to pin it to Ben's extra-wide lapel. "Hey, Johnny," she said, turning her head slightly in his direction. "I mean, 'John.'"

Johnny was taken aback. "Wow. That always amazes me when you do that. How'd you even know I was here?"

She smiled. "Actually, you kind of smell like ash."

Johnny sniffed the armpit of his tuxedo while Ben let out a loud guffaw. "Ash," he said, laughing.

Alicia was still trying to pin the flower on Ben's thick lapel. "Ow!" he yelled jokingly.

"Don't do that," she said, swatting him on the shoulder. She leaned into his rocky chest for a kiss. Johnny, feeling uncomfortable for intruding on their moment, looked down at his shoes.

"There," Alicia said, drawing her hands across his lapel. "Now you're perfect. I'll see you upstairs." She left the room, quietly closing the door behind her.

"So," Johnny said, trying to make small talk. "You and Alicia seem to be doing well. Annoyingly so, in fact."

"Yeah," Ben conceded. "I'm pretty lucky."

Johnny leaned in closer to his hulking, rocky friend and lowered his voice. "I'm just curious . . . how do you guys . . . you know . . ." He raised his eyebrows up and down to convey his meaning.

"That's none of your damn business!" Ben yelled, his hand curling into a fist.

Johnny backed off quickly. "Okay, okay. I'm just concerned. I mean, I'd hate to wake up one morning and find out she's been killed in a rock slide."

"I'll give *you* a rock slide," Ben said, moving closer, his fist still clenched.

Johnny let out a yelp. "Help! Monster! Grab your torches! Get your pitchforks!" Johnny ran out of the room with Ben in hot pursuit. He ran down the hallway and turned the corner. He ditched Ben by circling back to Reed's lab, where he was stopped dead in his tracks by the sight of his sister standing quietly in her long white gown, staring out at the rooftop deck. He walked over and joined her.

"Hey, it's the bride of Rubberman." His words were playful, but his tone was soft and tender.

Susan turned to face him. "Don't start," she said. Delicate lace framed her beautiful face.

"You know," Johnny began, taking her hand. "You don't look completely ridiculous in that dress."

She smiled at the compliment, knowing it was the

best he could give. "I assume that's obnoxious brother speak for *You look nice*."

"Pretty much," he said.

"Thanks," she said softly. She gave him a quick hug.

He pulled back, realizing that the ceremony was about to begin. "One more thing. Dad would have been proud of you."

The unexpected mention of their late father caught Sue off guard. Tears welled in her eyes and she planted a kiss on Johnny's cheek.

"Ewww!" he said playfully, just as the string quartet started to play. "Come on, let's do this thing! It's go-time!"

He took Sue's arm to lead his sister down the aisle, his eyes threatening to well up.

Outside, the weather was perfect for the ceremony. The entire roof was filled with friends and family eager to see the couple finally married. Reed surveyed the crowd, feeling his nerves disappear. He was ready to do this. The fragrance of flowers filled the air as he walked down the center aisle to where a minister was waiting under the domed wooden pergola. He was followed by Ben Grimm, who escorted Alicia down the aisle and to her chair before taking his place at Reed's side.

"I almost forgot," Reed whispered to him. "Do you have the ring?"

"Uh," Ben stammered. "Yeah," he said, glimpsing down into his rocky hand, which held a vaguely circular and damaged band.

Before Reed could react to his friend's hesitation, a short beeping sound came from the PDA in his coat pocket. He fumbled for it, pulling it out just as the screen flashed the words COSMIC RADIATION SURGE DETECTED. CALCULATING LOCATION AND TRAJECTORY.

"Reed," Ben whispered, "turn off your cell phone."

"Actually," Reed began, "this is a . . ."

He was interrupted by the string quartet, which started playing the wedding march. With the familiar music in the air, everyone stood, the eyes of all the guests turning to watch Susan Storm walk down the aisle, escorted by her handsome brother, Johnny. Reed put the PDA back in his pocket, excited at the arrival of his beautiful bride in her perfect dress.

"Dearly beloved," the minister began after the guests had once again taken their seats. "We are gathered here today to join this couple in holy matrimony." As the minister began his introduction, Reed slyly slid open his pocket flap to view the screen of his PDA. The display now read DESTINATION: NEW YORK, NY. CALCULATING TIME UNTIL IMPACT.

Sue noticed Reed's distraction and whispered angrily to him, "Reed! Did you actually bring that thing to our wedding?!"

"Yes," he whispered back. "But there's a good reason." He leaned in to the minister. "We need to get through this quickly."

"Oh, *that's* romantic," she said, narrowing her eyes, growing angrier.

The minister, obviously flustered by the famous couple arguing in front of him, tried a different tack. "There are many kinds of love—"

Reed nervously interrupted him again. "Could you skip to the end, please?"

"Excuse me?" the minister asked. They could all hear whispers coming from the rows of guests behind them.

The unobstructed view of the Manhattan skyline from the roof of the Baxter Building allowed everyone to see the thick and heavy clouds moving with unnatural speed across the city. Their dark, ominous color quickly covered Central Park in a midnight shadow. Soon the sun was all but covered, leading some to think they were witnessing the beginning of a solar eclipse. But the clouds were humming, expanding and contracting their form, pulsing with cosmic energy. A loud thunderclap boomed across the city, and fingers of electricity shot out from the clouds and struck the tops of several buildings on Central Park South as they moved closer to the Baxter Building. The wedding guests started eyeing one another nervously, wondering if their concern and growing fear were justified. The clouds looked like they were coming straight at them.

The minister raised his hand to quiet the murmuring crowd and continued. "Love is always patient and kind . . ." The shadow of the cloud reached the tip of the roof.

Reed stared down at his PDA. "Come on," he said to the minister. "Let's go, let's go . . ."

Sue's voice was rising in alarm and confusion. "Reed, what is wrong with you?"

As soon as the words left her mouth, a sudden gale swept over the entire roof. Silk scarves and decorative hats went flying, lost to the invisible and powerful winds. Tablecloths fluttered violently. Alicia gripped the sides of her chair fearfully. She could feel the strong winds and hear the murmuring around her. She thought she smelled fear.

Reed's PDA displayed the words LANDFALL IMMINENT. IMPACT IN 5 SECONDS. "Too late," was all Reed said, looking sadly at his bride. The display counted down slowly, each second seeming to linger.

The entire roof was now enveloped by the angry, threatening clouds. Lightning struck more often, extending its energy down around the roof. The sudden change in weather caught the helicopters circling the Baxter Building by surprise, exposing their vulnerability to the hostile winds; they were sitting ducks. A long piece of lightning lashed out against a news helicopter, blindsiding the pilot. The chopper fell from the air, heading straight for the rooftop and everyone at the wedding.

By now, the scene on the roof was sheer pandemonium. Guests were screaming and pointing, lost in the disarray caused by the electrical storm. Many gasped as they saw the copter falling toward the roof. The metal seemed to be screaming as the helicopter's silver belly smashed against the side of the building. Then it tipped forward, offering its main rotor blade to the guests, in a deadly somersault. The blade began chopping through the rows of empty seats left vacant by the terrified, fleeing guests. One couple, a man and his date, who was in a leg cast, huddled against each other, unable to move as quickly as the others. The man looked up the see the helicopter blade heading right for them. They hugged tightly and closed their eyes, prepared to meet their end.

Reed's outstretched arm quickly wrapped around them several times and jerked them out of harm's way. He watched them take cover inside his lab.

The chopper, eating through the wedding seats, rolled toward the pergola. The loud whir and constant wind were deafening. Sue saw the vehicle heading her way amid a flurry of debris and threw up a force field to protect herself. The copter banked off her shield and headed back toward the chairs, where a terrified Alicia sat, unable to move because she could not see where she should go. She felt the wind coming at her and knew the blade was heading directly for her.

Suddenly Ben leapt in front of her. The blade

grinded through his rocky chest, sending pebbles flying all over the floor of the roof. Impervious to its deadly sharp edges, Ben smashed his large, meaty fist through the blade and the entire tail of the helicopter, sending it skidding across the roof to the parapet wall, where it came to a rest. He turned to embrace Alicia, to hold her and protect her from the madness that was all around them.

The crowd ran from the roof, making their way out of the chaos and desperately wanting to get back to the streets below. In the confusion that ensued, no one noticed a figure inside the lab. It ignored the large object hovering under the cover of a plastic tarp, walking instead to a shadow-filled corner, approaching Reed's sensors for the antenna outside. Although almost completely in the dark, the figure continued to give off a reflected light. Two silver arms reached out to the sensor. One touch and the molecular structure of the arms began to change, transforming into pure crystal.

Outside, the rooftop deck was destroyed. Tables and chairs lay in chunks and ruins. Flowers, mostly in pieces, lay strewn around the ground. Sue picked up the tattered remnants of her wedding bouquet and surveyed the damage. Her heart sank as she fingered a large tear in her beautiful dress. She let the destroyed bouquet fall limply to the ground, joining the ruins of the day.

Ben, Reed, and Johnny were soon at her side, their faces still a picture of shock.

Johnny looked at his sister, standing there crest-fallen, her beautiful dress ruined. He, too, surveyed the damage all around them. He felt the anger rising in his chest. "Reed," he asked, "what the hell happened?"

"The source of the anomalies," he said darkly. "It's here."

Suddenly the silver object streaked past them, leaving the lab. It hovered above them, shining brightly against the dark, menacing clouds. The eyes of the Fantastic Four grew wide—above them floated a being seemingly made of pure silver, something in the shape of a man but obviously otherworldly, balanced on a sleek, thin board the same color as its skin. A chill ran through each of them as they realized that the thing they feared, the cause of the craters and molecular anomalies, was standing right in front of them.

6

THE FANTASTIC FOUR SEEMED TO BE HOLDING THEIR collective breath; they were transfixed by the form hovering above them. Reed's warning—*It's here*—still hung in the air, filling them all with a sense of trepidation. The silver figure eyed them warily, its cool skin reflecting the light. No one in the group could stop looking at it. The shock of the sudden storm, the ruined wedding, and the appearance of the silver figure had stalled their reactions.

Suddenly, the stalemate was broken. The silver figure turned and sped into the sky.

The group watched it streak quickly away from the Baxter Building and turn a corner, mixing into the Manhattan skyline, out of their sight.

Reed broke the silence. "Johnny . . ."

Johnny was right at his side. "I just bought this tux," he said pleadingly. But Reed's look was all business. Johnny ran toward the edge of the roof and jumped, casting his body into thin air. He yelled "Flame on!" and flames quickly covered his entire body, burning away the tux, turning him into living fire. He took off into the clearing sky, intent on following the silver object.

It didn't take long for Johnny to spot it. The silver man moved through the air with incredible speed, tearing around the skyline, dodging roofs and the sides of buildings, a trail of cosmic dust in his wake. Johnny was fast on his tail, heading due east, both of them soon coming upon the Chrysler Building, just west of the East River. Johnny's flames burned brighter as he neared the man, who was heading like a metallic missile right for the side of the historic building. He waved his hand, and the windows of the Chrysler Building changed right in front of his eyes. The windows rippled and moved like liquid, spreading open to form a hole. The silver figure soared through the opening and into the building without breaking one pane of glass. But just as quickly as the hole was created, it disappeared, once again becoming rigid metal and glass. Johnny, still moving at incredible speed, watched the building return to form and used all his strength to veer from his path, around the side of the building. "Son of a . . ." he muttered, catching a glimpse of the East River as he pulled himself back down toward the other side of the building just in time to see the figure emerge, the metal and glass once again rippling like water.

He then made an abrupt stop, right in midair. For the first time Johnny could get a clear look at his elusive prey. He felt his stomach drop at the sight. The figure, clearly the shape of a man, gleamed like a star atop the flying, shining board. Power and energy seemed to radiate from his being. His silver skin cast a brilliant hue, smooth and fluid, like liquid metal. His limbs moved gracefully atop the board, his form lithe and muscular. Surrounded by a city of metal and still the figure was radiant, almost celestial. Johnny couldn't help but think of some cosmic, shining, avenging angel.

Words escaped him, as they so often did, and all he could mutter was "Aw, that is *so* cool."

The silver man eyed him once again, his face stoic and blank. He then plunged downward, surfing on his board along the downward slope of the building. This time there were no ripples or changes, and the "Surfer's" violent downward plunge left a sea of shattered glass and twisted metal in its wake, falling around him to the streets below.

Johnny dived after him, incinerating as much debris as he could, fearing for the safety of the people at street level.

Their chase resumed as the silver figure sped through the city, banking on the sides of buildings and whipping around corners, leaving a trail of carnage in his wake. They backtracked over the island, toward the west side. From this height, Johnny could see the Empire State Building and other landmarks, bordered by the two rivers on either side of the wide strip of the heavily populated city.

The Surfer eyed a snakelike line of cars heading into the Lincoln Tunnel, an underwater throughway that connected New York to New Jersey. The burnished glare of the sunlight on the cars couldn't hold a torch to the shining silver man, who sped up as he raced smoothly into the two-lane underwater highway.

Inside the tunnel, the Surfer streaked over the traffic, cars moving quickly in the opposite direction, the lights of the tunnel exploding in his wake as he surged by. Johnny watched the lights explode, his burning body safe from the shards of glass, which incinerated upon contact with him. He burned brighter and started gaining ground on the figure as he continued to zig and zag around the upper reaches of the tunnel and the roofs of the moving cars. Sparks flew recklessly about. Startled drivers screeched to a halt, triggering a traffic bottleneck in the suddenly cramped and claustrophobic space. Johnny ignored them and flamed forward, squeezing between two cargo trucks. He was gaining on the Surfer, who had just come upon the back end of a commuter bus. The Surfer waved his hand and again the metal and glass rippled as he moved through the bus unharmed, the vehicle returning to form once he had passed through. Johnny almost crashed into the bus but once again at the last second pulled his body up and squeezed through the narrow pocket of space between the roof of the bus and the tunnel. The ensuing chase did not stop the speeding traffic, the cars grinding into one another as disoriented drivers tried to make sense of what they saw.

The Surfer slowed abruptly and paused. Johnny could see the Surfer begin to shine brighter as he inexplicably leaned forward and gracefully melted through his board. His body moved through the board like it was made of air, and then reformed on its underside. He began surfing upside down, regaining some of his speed. He looked back at a shocked Johnny and extended his hands. With one subtle gesture from the Surfer, cars took to the air and flew right into the path of the Human Torch. Johnny dodged the flying vehicles, trying to keep the destruction to a minimum. The sound of screeching and twisting metal was all around him, echoing in the crowded tunnel.

The Surfer then came upon a large flatbed truck hauling pallets of wood. He once again flicked his hand and the pallets snapped off the truck, rising into the air. They formed a grid of crossing beams, a patchwork wall, right in front of Johnny. He burned his flame higher, hoping to burn through the wood, but it was too late. He smashed through the flying wall, the wood hitting his body with hard, loud *thwacks*. The pallets battered his body savagely; Johnny could feel the pain coursing through him as pieces of wood showered the traffic below. The cars tried to stop too quickly and went spinning in the narrow lanes of traffic, the loud squealing of their brakes and collisions adding noise to the already intensely loud chamber. Johnny clutched his side—did he break a rib?—skidding and bouncing against the walls of the tunnel, leaving a trail of flames behind him.

He righted himself again, still clutching his side, just in time to see the Surfer melt back up through his board. Both figures seemed to draw deep breaths, steadying their nerves, before increasing their speed and shooting out of the tunnel and into the air above New Jersey.

Johnny's flames still burned brightly, but his speed was tremendous. The Surfer was indefatigable. Johnny continued to chase the Silver Surfer over the eastern seaboard, past the landscapes of forests and countrysides. He kept the Atlantic Ocean to his left so he wouldn't lose his sense of direction as the world blurred by. Soon landmarks presented themselves. They chased over the nation's capital, the metallic Surfer whizzing by in stark contrast to the large white edifices. He whipped around the Washington Monument, his powerful wake of energy and dust causing the tall white structure to crack. Johnny followed, growing angrier with the endless pursuit. He thought of everything he'd seen today: the terrified drivers in the tunnel, the destruction of the buildings and property back in Manhattan, and, most of all, the broken-hearted look on his sister's face at her ruined wedding, the dying bouquet of flowers falling limply from her hand. His rage increased his flame. *Come on*, he said to himself, *you can take this guy*. In the back of his mind he also thought *This one's for Sue*.

Johnny pulled his hand in front of him and unleashed a fireball toward the Surfer. The swirling, concentrated mass of flame burned more white than orange, a weapon borne of Johnny's intense emotional state. It hit the Surfer squarely in his back and Johnny could see the tremble move through him, his feet suddenly wobbly on the board.

The silver figure turned around to face Johnny, stopping itself in midair. Johnny, all flame and inertia, could not stop in time. The Surfer reached out and grabbed him like a child choosing a toy, one hand tight around Johnny's neck. The Surfer held Johnny tightly on the board and began raising them both high into the air.

Even in full flame, Johnny could feel the energy of the being pulsing through him. It was unlike anything he had ever felt, a sense of vertigo and nausea and power that he was trying to overcome him, to take control of him.

Johnny struggled to get away, to be released from the being's otherworldly grip, but he could not budge. "Okay," he said. "Let's see what it takes to melt that silver butt of yours."

Johnny poured on the heat, using everything within him to burn brighter and brighter. He quickly approached supernova, the dangerous state Reed had always warned him about, the type of fury and power he'd used to help defeat Victor Von Doom. He could feel the flames in every part of his being, down to his core, burning away the feelings of relinquishing control. But the Surfer was unaffected. His strength remained constant, unmoving, uncaring. He maintained his savage grip on Johnny and continued to rise higher and higher into the air.

Johnny saw the blue sky begin to fade and dim. The black edge of space came into fuzzy focus. The distant light of small silver stars appeared on the horizon, mimicking the form that held him tightly. From this vantage point, Johnny could see the beginning of outer space and beyond, the finite edges of the Earth and its surrounding atmosphere. The power of the silver figure and its board still surged through him, once again infiltrating his mind. His own flame, in the thin oxygen, grew dangerously low. He could not draw breath and began to extinguish. Suddenly he was face-to-face with the silver figure, drifting on the cusp of space and consciousness. He began to feel his own life dimming. He had been to space before, but it hadn't felt like this. A feeling of isolation overtook him; he felt dwarfed by the ethereal figure of the Surfer and the looming heavens of space, and the thin air was making his mind feel clouded and confused. His last thought was of Earth: How majestic it appeared to be against the deep sea of black space, how lonely it looked in such a great expanse.

"Uh . . . you win?" Johnny finally managed to get out.

The Surfer released Johnny from his grip. The limp figure of Johnny Storm plummeted from the upper skies, falling like a piece of unwanted debris back down to Earth. He tried to regain his composure, stifling the screams that were welling up inside him. The free fall seemed to take forever, and yet no time at all. "Flame on!" He tried to reignite his body, but to no avail. He was too shaken up, still reeling from his encounter with the dangerous and enigmatic Surfer.

The hardscape of land was coming fast upon him. Just as he was about to hit, something in the back of his mind snapped. "Flame on flame on flame on flame on—!" and suddenly they were with him again, his entire body turning to fire. He tried to pull up from his deep descent but it was too late. The flames provided some measure of protection as he went skidding across a rough-hewn patch of dirt, dead grass, and rocks. He bounced and tumbled, once again grabbing the sore side of his torso. In a cloud of dust and dirt, Johnny finally, gratefully, came to a halt.

The dust settled and parted, and Johnny found himself flat on his back. He opened his eyes, waving away the dust and dirt around him. As he stood up gingerly, pain surged through his side and left leg. He checked himself, making sure nothing was broken. Looking over at the sound of an animal, he saw a herd of cattle staring right at him, their dull, glassy eyes unimpressed with his descent from heaven.

Two old gauchos on horseback sat nearby. Their eyes were less dull, a bit wide from what they had just witnessed. One started to applaud.

"Where the hell am I?" Johnny asked.

The gauchos stopped clapping; one of them spat out a glob of tobacco and said, "Mexico."

"Great," Johnny said, limping away from the smell of the dirt and the animals, back on the surface of the planet but not feeling much better for it.

7

REED'S LAB ONCE AGAIN HUMMED WITH ACTIVITY. The ruins of the attempted wedding were still scattered across the roof deck and were now being blown around by a lazy and uninterested wind. The media down on the street had long ago dispersed. Pieces of chairs and tables lay where they had all day, fallen victims in the field of battle. A flower or two decorated the space before they, too, bowed their heads and fell silent. Sue couldn't look at it any longer. She steered clear of the windows and their view.

Ben stood motionless in the corner of the room. He had been that way since the electrical storm, his mind likley replaying the sight of his precious Alicia in the path of the helicopter.

A crowd had once again gathered, this one starkly different from the wedding guests that only hours before had filled the space. The military had flooded the lab, eager to learn as much as they could about the Four's close encounter with the silver being. Even Captain Raye couldn't keep her eyes off Johnny as he stood before them, telling them the details of what happened.

"It looked like a man," Johnny continued. "But it was completely covered in silver. And it was flying on top of a . . . a surfboard-type thing. I know that sounds a little crazy."

Ben shook the thoughts of Alicia from his head to catch the end of Johnny's story. "Crazy? No, not at all. So did you follow the shiny man to Lollipop Land or Rainbow Junction?"

"Look, I know what I saw!" Johnny said. *That thing almost killed me and no one seems to care.*

"Thank you, Johnny," Reed said. "It's all right. Whatever this thing's physical appearance is, it had the ability to convert matter and energy."

General Hager cleared his throat and spoke up. "So it caused the anomalies?"

Reed nodded his head. "It seems to radiate cosmic energy when it exerts itself, randomly affecting matter. Evidently, this entity, this . . ."

"Silver Surfer," Johnny interjected.

"*Silver Surfer*," Reed allowed, "doesn't want to be detected. It destroyed the sensor."

"It knew it was being monitored?" Sue asked.

Reed nodded again. "And tracked it back here. We're dealing with something highly resourceful."

Johnny tried to follow the conversation but still wasn't feeling like himself after his encounter with the Silver Surfer. His stomach was in knots and he couldn't shake the feeling of being suspended in the outer reaches of the Earth's atmosphere, where it was cold—cold enough to extinguish his flame. Where he felt so helpless and alone.

Sue walked over to him. She went to place her hand on his shoulder but he flinched and pulled back. "Johnny, are you okay?"

He looked at his sister's face. Concern etched lines into her brow. She looked so tired. He wanted to tell her all about it, his encounter with the silver thing, and how it made him feel. But he couldn't.

"Yeah, I think I just need to walk it off." He turned and walked slowly toward the elevator banks.

General Hager was staring at Reed. "We need to destroy that thing before it attacks again. Richards, find me another way to track it."

Ben still didn't like the general's tone of voice. "A 'please' would be nice."

The exasperated general's stare could have bored holes into Ben's rocky face. "If you want to protect the people you care about, you should get your priorities straight. *Please*." The words stung even Ben's hide as he once again thought about Alicia and how close he'd come to losing her. He barely noticed Hager and the rest of the military leave the laboratory.

The words apparently left an impression on Reed as well. He walked over to Sue, who still seemed to be avoiding the wreckage of their wedding. "Sue, I'm so sorry," Reed said. "I had no idea the sensor would bring that thing here. The only reason I didn't tell you about it is because I didn't want you to worry."

She reached out and touched his cheek. "Reed, I'm not mad that you built the sensor. It was the right thing to do."

"Oh, then great!" he said. He started to walk away from her and back to his work, but she threw a force field in front of him. He slammed right into it. Then he felt another field right behind him. Sue pushed the two fields together, trapping Reed, exerting such pressure on him that he started to thin out his body. She spun him around so he was facing her.

"I wasn't finished," she said calmly, a fire in her eyes.

"Oh, sorry," Reed said. "Please, continue."

Ben could sense a storm coming. He wanted to get the hell out of there, maybe go check on Alicia. "I'm going to grab a sandwich," he said, exiting the room quickly.

Sue ignored Ben and focused all her energy on Reed, keeping him trapped tightly between the two fields. "This just proves what I've been saying all along."

"Would you drop the force-fields, please?" he asked. After a moment's hesitation Sue complied, and Reed quickly reformed his body to his normal shape. "Thank you."

Sue's anger was undiminished. "We can't even get through a wedding without it turning into World War Three. How can we possibly raise a family like this? Face it—we can't do what we do and lead normal lives. You know it's true."

Reed looked at her, slightly stunned.

Out of the corner of her eye, Sue thought she saw a sudden flash of color through the large windows. A blur of orange and red. Her brother? She said, "I'm going to check on Johnny."

Sue pushed through the revolving doors of the Baxter Building and out onto the street. She spied her brother, obviously dazed, keeping his balance by holding on to a nearby lamppost. A small crowd of worried onlookers was beginning to gather around him, keeping a safe distance. Flames shot upward from his body even though he was not ignited.

"Johnny!" Sue yelled out to him, concerned at the strange sight. "What's wrong?"

Johnny looked at his sister, fear staining his face. "I don't know. I've been feeling weird ever since my run-in with Surfer boy."

"Okay," she said, trying to take control of the situation. "Maybe we should take you to a . . ."

Before Sue could complete her sentence, Johnny looked up at her. He grabbed her arm and she jumped at his sudden and rather fearsome grip. His eyes burned silver. As Sue started to scream, a wave of cosmic energy leapt out of her brother and bathed her in its radiant glow. The powerful energy bombarded Sue, flooding her entirely with strange sensations and emotions, and was soon refracted back at Johnny, the two held captive by the ethereal bioluminescence.

Sue stepped back from her brother, dazed and confused. Suddenly her entire body burst into flames. She started slapping at her arms, trying to extinguish the fire.

"Johnny," she yelled. "What did you do that for?!"

But Johnny looked as confused as his sister. He could barely speak. "I didn't do anything!" he stammered. "Stop, drop, and roll, Sis!" Sue did as he said, but could not extinguish the flames. Strangely, she could not feel the heat on her skin. She watched helplessly as the flames burned brighter, hotter, making her body rise off the street. "Stop, drop, and roll!"

"What's happening?!" she shouted, her body just reaching the top of the lamppost.

"Hang on," Johnny said. "I'll get you! Flame on!"

But instead of igniting his body, Johnny's efforts turned him invisible. A passing stranger walked into him, knocking Johnny down. "Hey, watch it!" A few others passed by quickly, bumping into and tripping over him. It took him a moment to realize what had happened. He held his hand in front of his face and saw the light ripple against nothing. "What the hell . . . ? this is so not right," he said, his voice sounding small as he watched his sister rise away from him.

Upstairs in his lab, Reed had pushed aside his doubts about Sue to focus on finding the Silver Surfer. Hager was right—he had to find this thing in order to protect his family.

He was typing into his PDA, trying to figure out another way to track the silver being, when he saw a flaming figure floating outside his window. Reed jumped back, a bit surprised. "Johnny," he said. "You scared the hell out of me."

"I'm not Johnny!" the figure shouted.

Reed recognized the voice. "Sue?" he asked, startled. The figure started to descend and Reed did the same, taking the elevator down to the lobby. He ran out onto the street, where he found his flaming fiancé hovering just above the ground. Reed could also see passersby bumping into something unseen and a voice that sounded like Johnny's repeatedly saying "Ouch."

The pedestrians pointed up at Sue, as if a person on fire was a familiar thing to see in New York City. "Hey, it's the Human Torch," one yelled. Another exclaimed, "No, it's a girl!" and yet another said, "He's so cute."

"No," Sue protested, waving her flaming hands in the air. "I'm not. I mean, I am, but . . . look, just go away!"

Johnny was eager to greet his fans but no one could see him. His protests couldn't change that fact. "Over here, ladies!" he yelled fruitlessly. "Look at me, over here!" His exclamations fell upon deaf ears. Johnny gave up, defeated. "This is my worst nightmare."

Reed went running at the sound of Johnny's voice. "Sue?! How did this happen?"

Sue floated down toward him. "I have no idea. I touched Johnny, and then this!"

"Where *is* Johnny?" Reed asked.

"Here." Johnny walked toward him, fading in and out of sight, a ripple in the air. "What's happening?" he asked Reed.

Reed rubbed his chin, thinking. "You said your powers switched when you touched? Try it again."

Johnny reached up to touch his sister. As soon as he made contact, a wave of cosmic energy leapt out of him and once again bathed her in its radiance. The powerful energy bombarded Sue and was soon refracted back at Johnny, as before.

Johnny became visible again and ignited his hand to prove his point. "Cool! Hey, I'm back!"

He looked to the now staring and confused crowd for support, but all eyes were locked on his sister. Her body had lost its flames, but in the switch all of her clothes had been burned off. Without the benefit of her special suit, she was left naked in the light of day. It took a second for Sue to realize what had happened. She turned herself invisible once again to hide from the prying, wide eyes of the crowd. "Why does this always happen to me?" she asked no one in particular.

Reed herded them back inside the Baxter Building. He was now faced with yet another facet of the silver entity's strange effect on this planet and its inhabitants. *It has the ability to manipulate their powers?* Reed feared what was to come next. For if even their special abilities were at the mercy of this Silver Surfer, he feared they didn't have a prayer of defeating it.

8

THE FOLLOWING DAY THE FANTASTIC FOUR SOMBERLY gathered in Reed's lab, their collective minds clouded and concerned. The events of the previous day—the ruined wedding, their encounter with the Silver Surfer, and the unexpected switching of their special abilities on the street—made for a sorrowful mood. Sue kept to the corners, watching Reed at work and still trying to avoid the sight of the wedding mess outside. Ben stood solidly by Reed's side, the way he always did, feeling a bit better having spent some time last night with Alicia, who'd finally convinced him she was fine. Johnny was fidgety and restless, more than freaked out after yesterday's fight with the Surfer and his time spent invisible. No one would say it out loud, but everyone was keeping a safe distance from him, fearful of another unexpected transformation, and that compounded Johnny's lingering feelings of isolation.

Reed was too busy looking for an explanation for yesterday's power switch to notice the brooding, moody demeanor of his group. He placed his faith in science, not in feeling, and he knew there had to be a plausible explanation as to what had happened. He felt it had to have something to do with the Surfer, since that was the only new element in the mix. But, as he hated to admit, he knew painfully little about the real makeup of their powers. He could trace and isolate their DNA and prove beyond a doubt that it was the cosmic space storm that had altered them on a basic molecular level, thereby giving them their special abilities. *But,* he wondered, *could those alterations somehow be temporary? Could the body, seeking to right itself, somehow find a way around to switching the DNA back to its original state?* He'd never thought about the long-term effects and ramifications of their powers before; he was always too busy with the here and now to think much about the future. Suddenly, that seemed like just another one of his mistakes.

Reed peered into the electromagnetic telescope. He had been comparing samples from Sue and Johnny, looking for clues. He pulled back from the scope, rubbing his eyes. "All of Sue's results are normal," he said finally, casting a glance in her direction. "But Johnny's . . ."

"But Johnny's what?" Johnny asked, his voice laced with panic.

Reed swallowed hard and looked at the impetuous young man, whom he already thought of as a brother. "Your encounter with the Surfer must have affected you somehow. Your molecules seem to be in a constant state of flux."

Johnny took a moment to digest the information, not that he seemed to understand what most of it meant. "Is that bad?" he asked.

Reed wasn't sure. "It caused you to temporarily switch powers with Sue. We should do a test and see if it happens again."

Sue was already shaking her head when Ben stepped up. "You need a volunteer?"

"No, no. Stay back," Johnny protested.

"C'mere," Ben said playfully. "I just want to give you a hug."

"Get back!" Johnny said, putting his arms in front of him. "Somebody stop him."

Johnny's pleas went unheeded, as Ben reached out for him. As soon as they touched, a wave of cosmic energy leapt out of Johnny and covered Ben in its furious glow. The powerful energy bombarded Ben and was soon refracted back at Johnny, as with Sue the day before. Ben's rocky hide diminished and he once again took on the appearance of being human, like he had been before the storm. His human form then began to ignite, turning him into a living flame.

"Not bad," he said, admiring the fire.

But Johnny didn't fare so well. He ran over to a mirror to see his features shifting and changing into the rocky visage of what he'd once mockingly called the Thing. He was heavy and slow; the density of his new shape weighing him down. "I'm in hell," he said, putting his fist through a wall.

"Welcome to my world," Ben said, making small rings of fire in the air around him.

Reed watched the interchange, a bit fascinated by the impressive display of cosmic energy if not by their rapid transformations. It occurred exactly as he'd thought it would. "I'm sorry, Johnny," he said. "You'll just have to wait until I can find a cure."

But Johnny wasn't having any of it. "I can't keep switching my powers with you guys," he protested. "I *like* my powers. And your powers *suck*." Suddenly, a fireball smashed into his rocky hide. Even with his newly thick skin, the burst of fire hurt. "Ouch!"

Ben stood behind him, laughing through his flames. "I'm starting to see why you think that's so funny."

Before Ben could utter another word, Johnny reached out and grabbed his flaming arm. The physical contact once again triggered the transformation of powers, the illuminating switch lighting up the lab. Johnny reverted to his normal form as Ben once again took on the rocky appearance of the Thing.

Satisfied that his features were as they should be, Johnny turned back to Reed. "What am I supposed to do in the meantime?"

"Just try to keep your distance from us," Reed responded.

Ben spoke up. "You and me are going to be spending a lot of time together, pal!"

Johnny grimaced at the remark and took a few steps back from the laughing pile of rock.

Sue had quietly left the laboratory, not wanting to watch her brother and Ben goad each other over the switching of their powers. She felt tired of their constant teasing and games. Her head hurt, and she still couldn't bring herself to go out to the rooftop deck, though she figured someone should start to clean up the mess. A few helicopters had passed by this morning, now that the weather had cleared and returned to normal, to photograph the wreckage. She didn't want any more of their dirty laundry aired on national TV. And yet the mess seemed to serve as justification for everything she was feeling: She could never be normal. She could never be truly invisible, fading from the limelight.

She absentmindedly flipped on the television, hoping to find out if there was any news of the Surfer. Instead, she saw a photo of her own roof, the damage looking far worse from above. An entertainment reporter was expounding on the mayhem and destruction caused by yet another failed wedding attempt, and the panic that the storms had caused on the streets. She saw bloodied figures, many of them her own wedding guests, being helped by police and paramedics. She saw the terrified faces of normal people running away from the Baxter Building as the skies turned black, as the helicopter pitched itself onto the roof.

Oblivious to the grave images, the reporter continued to speak: "That's right. It was another 'Fantastic Flop' of a wedding! Inside sources say the unlucky, would-be bride Sue Storm turned invisible and she's *staying* that way after yesterday's embarrassing fiasco. Coming up next, the Invisible Woman's greatest fashion blunders . . ."

Tears formed in the corners of Sue's eyes as the anger swelled in her stomach. Reed, who had been standing behind her, walked over to the set and turned it off. "It's garbage," he said softly. "Just ignore it."

But Sue was beyond comforting. "I can't just ignore it! This is what our lives are now. There's no getting away from it!" Her raised voice cracked with her feelings of frustration and hurt.

She knew broke Reed's heart to see her like this. For all the media attention that their powers brought them, Reed never thought much about the lasting effects. He could always slink away and return to his lab, oblivious to the outside world. He dismissed the media the same way he dismissed Johnny's obvious love of it—as a toy that could be played with and then put away whenever one wanted. He had never really thought about how much Sue struggled with it.

Her obvious beauty made her the most public face of the group, even with Johnny's insatiable need for attention. But she was the only woman here, and he'd probably never before realized how much of a target that made her.

"Yes, there is," he said.

He reached out for her. She struggled a bit, but he held her fast. Could he make it different for her?

"After this crisis is over," he began, looking deep into her pained eyes, "we'll leave it all behind. We will move out of the Baxter Building. I'll take a teaching position somewhere, get back to doing serious research. And the two of us will live our lives and raise a family like normal people." He touched her cheek.

Sue looked up. "You'd do that?"

He played with a lock of her long blond hair. "We don't have a choice," he said.

Sue held him, not quite believing her ears. Tears slid down her cheeks. It was everything she wanted him to say. *For once.* So why did it hurt so much? "It's going to hit Johnny and Ben hard," she said.

"They'll understand," Reed said. "Besides, Johnny's always been more of a solo act."

Sue let out a small laugh, still not believing they were actually having this conversation. She wiped the tears from her face. If she'd ever needed proof of Reed's love for her, she had it now. She felt it. "Let's not mention it to them now," she said. "Johnny's got enough to worry about as it is."

"I think we *all* do," he said in reply. They held each other in their embrace, lost in their own thoughts, silently confirming that it was time to bring about the end of the Fantastic Four.

9

THE SPRAWLING ICE SHEETS OF GREENLAND STRETCHED for miles in every direction, white upon white, as far as the eye could see. Its absence of color was one of the country's most startling attributes, here at the top of the world, where the aberrant weather and the isolation had driven many a pilot or explorer to the brink of insanity. The constancy of the ice and the absence of color created feelings of both vertigo and confusion. From every direction the view looked the same, causing many to lose their bearings—and their minds. Victor Von Doom knew this, had read the many accounts of academic experiments gone wrong here. So he had come prepared.

Victor swung his helicopter to the right, surveying the endless expanse of white, the sun fueling a reflective glare that could easily blind him. The view shield to the copter had been fitted with a special tint that defrayed most of the glare, making his passage easier. The craft was also outfitted with the latest GPS technology and satellite direction, thereby reducing his chances of becoming lost. Victor had been asleep in that crate for who knew how long, and he didn't welcome the idea of another unexpected nap, deep in the ice.

Victor adjusted his coordinates and slowed his speed. He scratched an itch on the side of his burned and damaged face, wincing at the pain. He feared his face was beyond repair, another lingering effect of the cosmic storm that had irrevocably changed his life, so he left it open to the elements. The infamous family faceplate remained in his laboratory in Latveria. *This mission requires a bit more finesse*, he thought, even with the backup firepower he carried to make sure his brute strength was more than understood. He pulled his green cowl up over his head against the dipping temperatures of the barren landscape.

Overhead, one of his sensors blinked a warning red, the quiet beeping filling the cockpit. "There you are," he said, adjusting his flight path accordingly. It felt good to be back on the hunt.

The wide, opaque glacier pointed like a finger from the Earth to the sky. It was the highest peak in the surrounding area of this frozen wasteland, its base sometimes obscured by the gusty winds and ice flurries common to the region. In the middle of the ice sheet sat a deep crater. There was no residual debris to suggest the crater was the work of an asteroid hitting the Earth, and the surrounding ice showed no signs of deep impact. The crater was perfectly round and smooth, its flawless walls glistening silver, leading down deep from the face of the ice sheets. A glow rose from the crater, bathing it in a light that was clearly not of this world.

Inside the crater, the alien being rotated on his board, his hands outstretched. The mere motion of his hand turned the earthen walls into the smooth, silvery material, reinforcing the crater and rounding it in its luminescence. The being's face was passive, stoic, unaffected by his task and almost robotic in its execution.

Victor Von Doom exited his sleek helicopter just a few feet from the glowing crater. He walked carefully toward it, his long green cowl blowing behind him in the icy wind. The alien paused and turned his head, as if listening for something. He began to rise, the board effortlessly taking its rider out of the deep crater to the surface of the ice above.

Victor shielded his eyes, shards of ice from the alien's exit flying at him like broken glass, his powerful metallic arms keeping him safe. He stared at the alien, fascinated. Its long, sleek body seemed to be made entirely of a silver alloy. The radiant glow seemed to come from within him, not relying on the sun for the reflection of light. It glistened with power, standing sturdy atop his flying board. Victor was almost humbled. *He doesn't look that different from me*, Victor thought. The alien, too, seemed confused by the similarity and stood motionless, hanging in the air.

Victor turned his gaze from the alien to the crater

he had just made. "Don't tell me," he said mockingly, his scarred face even more twisted as he tried to smile. "It's the world's biggest barbecue pit."

The alien remained still, staring impassively at Victor. His face showed neither acknowledgment nor concern.

"No?" Victor continued. "Honestly, I don't really care what it is. I came here to make you an offer. Do you understand what I'm saying?" Victor said the last words slowly, as if speaking to a child.

The alien nodded his head.

Victor smiled. He could communicate with this thing. *Good*, he thought. *Let's hope it understands the universal language of power.* "Together, we could be unstoppable. Anything would be ours for the taking!" Victor clenched his fist by his side, his metallic hand closing, an expression of his power. He stared at the alien, waiting for an answer to his offer. He knew that with this being at his side, it would be only a matter of time before the entire world would be squirming under his foot. He could at last begin to take back everything he'd lost.

The alien continued to hover in the air. Nothing about the appearance of Victor or his offer caused a change: His body, his face, his physical language were silent, stoic, unaltered. Without any change in expression, the alien started to speak. His voice carried a slight tremble and an otherworldly depth.

"*All that you know is at an end.*"

Victor stared at the alien's face, a blank silver slate. He was unable to read it. "What do you mean by that?" Victor asked. He was prepared for violence if, indeed, that was a threat.

The alien raised his hand and made a simple hand gesture. As if on cue, the ice sheet beneath Victor cracked like glass and broke away. Victor stumbled on the hard ice, into the small valley made by the alien. The silent silver being started to move away.

"Wait!" Victor shouted, recovering from the fall and shaking ice from his metallic arms.

The silver being ignored Victor, continuing to move away.

Victor's patience was at an end. Alien or not, nothing in this world or any other ignored him. "I said *wait!*" he bellowed, unleashing a torrent of electricity from his hands toward the being. The fingers of power reflected in the ice sheets below as they staggered and danced all over the alien's body. The powerful glare from the blast covered them both, blinding Victor for just an instant.

He recovered his sight to see the alien hovering as before, unaffected by Victor's powerful blast. His stoic silver face showed no sign of pain or concern.

Victor experienced a moment of panic. The charge he'd hit the creature with could have leveled a building. *What the hell am I dealing with?* he thought.

The alien raised a hand. Victor felt a tugging deep inside him, as if something was trying to claw its way out of his body. He clutched his chest, metal hitting metal, as his legs began to shiver and shake. The last thing he saw was an endless expanse of white: either the sky or the ground, or the distant horizon beyond. Victor was pulled apart into billions of tiny particles of matter. It happened so quickly that he did not feel a thing. The alien kept the particles floating there above the ice, the last remnants of Victor Von Doom, hovering like fireflies. With another flick of his hand, the alien sent them sailing away upon the icy wind like so many motes of dust.

The particles continued flying on the air and went sailing through a wall of solid ice, far away from the alien's crater, into a cave. The darkness inside the cave was not helped by the presence of thick walls of ice surrounding its exterior that only reflected light away from the cold, dank space. The particles entered the cave and hovered, as if shivering in the cold. One by one they slowly gathered together, reforming the person of Victor Von Doom. Victor, reassembled, fell to the floor of the cave. He clutched his stomach and tried to retch into the cold, dark ice but nothing came. He breathed deeply and quickly, trying to calm his quaking mind, his rage balanced only by a small sense of awe at the power of the silver being.

"Aliens," Victor said, spitting the word out like a

curse. He dragged his body up from the ice floor, limping slightly, staggering to find an exit. His metallic body moved slowly, but his mind was a flurry of activity. If this silver being could rip him apart with one slight gesture, Victor realized, he needed to use more than brute strength to stop him. *Yes*, he thought, he would need something a bit more cerebral. Which meant it was time to pay a visit to some old friends.

10

JOHNNY STORM STOOD FROZEN, AS IF ENTOMBED IN ice. Barely visible in the dimly lit hallway, he placed his cheek against the wall. It felt cool against his burning skin, but it was not enough to quell the firestorm inside him. He backed slowly, away from the partially opened door and his sister and Reed faded from his view. The slightly charred doorframe gave off a hint of smoke, but it disappeared quickly. As did Johnny.

His mind raced as he made his way back to his room. He couldn't believe his sister wanted to disband the group. And because of what? Some stupid reporters? How many times had he told her to ignore them, to just smile and not answer their questions? *They're looking to goad you*, he lectured her repeatedly, *to sell more newspapers. That's their job.* But her skin was too thin. He knew that. He liked to think that part of the reason he hogged the spotlight was so that she could rest a bit more easily and slip away from the glare of the media. *She isn't strong*, he thought. *Not like me.*

Johnny kept walking, his mind replaying the conversation he had just heard: Reed and Sue were going to leave the group. He should have confronted them both, right then and there. But then they'd know he'd been eavesdropping again, something he'd promised them both he would stop doing. But this was bigger than a mere prank or an invasion of privacy—much bigger. Quit the group? Johnny was caught so off guard at hearing the words that he felt speechless, perhaps for the first time. *Better to cool off a bit,* he thought, *cool off and come back with a logical and rational explanation for why disbanding the Fantastic Four is a bad idea. One that doesn't even make financial sense.*

Johnny rounded the corner and heard voices coming from Ben's room. The door was slightly ajar, a thin strip of light extending into the hallway. He crept closer to the voices, one deep and rocky, the other much less so.

Inside Ben's room, Alicia placed her hands deep in the soft clay. Her long, delicate digits traveled slowly over the smooth material, their tips putting pressure where she needed to mold and form the shape.

One hand left the clay, venturing out into the empty space like a new bird, fearful of flight. Her fingers pushed through the open air until she touched Ben's face. Ben smiled. Johnny would never admit it, but he liked that there was something that could make Ben smile like that. Alicia's sculptures were refined and careful, delicate, and never severe. Johnny was impressed that she could make even something like Ben worth looking at.

"Stop smiling," Alicia said.

Ben's smile widened. "You're tickling me."

"Should I hit you with a hammer?" she asked.

"That would just tickle more," he replied.

Johnny couldn't take another second of this.

He stormed into the room. Alicia and Ben looked startled, which Johnny ignored. He wanted action. "They're breaking up the team!" he said loudly.

"What?" Ben asked.

"Reed and Sue," Johnny said. "They're going to drop out of to have a nice, normal, boring-ass life. No more Fantastic Four. I just overheard them talking about it."

"You were spying on them?" Alicia asked quietly.

Johnny was incredulous. Even Alicia was missing the point. "What's worse, spying or breaking up the freakin' team?"

His question hung in the silence of the room as each of them thought about what Reed and Sue's decision could mean. Alicia harbored a small glimmer of hope that such a thing could be true, she knew she and Ben would never be considered a normal couple, but there was no reason for Ben to continue to stand so obviously in harm's way. Her brush with death on the roof of this very building had only cemented her fear of someone getting hurt—seriously hurt. She never told Ben how much she feared for his safety, for all of the Four's safety. Now, maybe she wouldn't have to.

Thoughts tumbled like rocks in Ben's mind. He couldn't believe that Reed would make such a big decision without him, but his feelings for Sue often made Reed do things Ben couldn't anticipate. Maybe this was one of those times. Finally he spoke up. "Do they expect us to keep things going with just the two of us?"

"And call ourselves what? *The Dynamic Duo?* You know how lame that sounds?" Johnny asked heatedly. His emotions were running high. He didn't understand why Ben wasn't as angry as he was.

"When were they going to tell us?" Ben asked.

"Maybe when the movers showed up to haul our stuff out of the Baxter Building," Johnny replied angrily.

Alicia put her hand on Ben's massive arm. "They'll come to you when they're ready. But this is *their* decision, not yours. You can't be mad at them if this is what they need to be happy."

Johnny wasn't listening to her. She wasn't part of the group—she didn't understand. "But *I'm* happy *now*," he said. As soon as he finished the sentence, he realized how childish he sounded, but he didn't care.

Before Ben could respond, they all heard footsteps in the hallway. Reed entered the room swiftly, oblivious to the tension in the room. His face were a somber expression. "Guys," he said, "we have a serious problem."

Ben looked at him. "You bet we do. We need to talk."

Reed dismissed Ben's comment. "Not now," he said. "Follow me."

Ben and Johnny were silenced by the grim tone in Reed's voice. They could both sense that something important had come up. Everything else would have to wait.

Johnny and Ben followed Reed into his laboratory. They were surprised to see that General Hager, Captain Raye, and their usual military escort were already waiting there. Reed ignored the group in the room and walked directly to his computer and started punching in numbers. Johnny surveyed the crowd and walked over to the attractive Captain Raye. She looked up at him and smiled. *Finally*, Johnny thought. *I'm making some headway*. Raye was holding a copy of the *New York Post* and flipped the newspaper over, revealing its front page. The paper featured a full-page cover shot of Johnny, down on one knee, handing flowers to Ben. Johnny remembered the shot from the many errands he and Ben had done for Reed before the latest ruined wedding attempt. The headline of the paper read "JUST Fantastic Friends?" Raye met his look with a wry grin.

"That's not what it looks like," Johnny said, stumbling over his words and feeling himself blush.

"It's none of my business," Captain Raye said quickly.

"Sure it is!" Johnny countered. "It's *completely* your business." But Raye simply shrugged her shoulders and walked away, once again taking her place at the imposing side of General Hager.

The general was in his usual sour mood, his face creased into its customary scowl. "What's the emergency, Richards?"

Reed looked up from his computer and addressed the group. "I've been cross-referencing the Surfer's radiation through every astronomical database." He pointed to a large monitor to his right and scrolled through a series of satellite photos of dead and barren planets not far from Earth's solar system. Each photo was worse than the one before, showing lifeless landscapes, dried-up oceans, and ruined atmospheres. It all looked boring to Johnny. "Altair Seven. Rigel Three . . . Vega Six." Reed fell silent, letting the pictures speak for themselves.

Ben looked stunned. "He's been to all those planets?"

Reed nodded his head solemnly. "And now they're lifeless, barren. No atmosphere, no thermal activity, nothing. Wherever the Surfer goes—eight days later, the planet dies."

Sue spoke up. "He's already been here for six days."

Johnny was finally catching on. "Are you saying if we don't stop it in the next forty-eight hours, there will be nothing left alive?"

Once again, Reed nodded. Everyone in the room started murmuring and whispering, expressing their shock and dismay. A heavy mood fell over the crowd as each person came to terms with the grim and frightening news.

"Get me the White House," General Hager ordered Captain Raye, who immediately pulled out her cell phone and started dialing. That one small act seemed to shake the room's occupants from their collective shock.

"How do we stop him?" Ben asked, sounding ready for a fight. "We don't even know where to find him."

Reed turned back to his computer and punched up a display of Earth on the screen. "The Surfer's craters are marked with those blinking dots," he said.

Sue walked over to his side. "The craters?"

Reed continued. "They seem random, but there's something about them . . ." He thought for a moment, then hit a button on the console that rotated the image of Earth. The dots indicating the craters disappeared for a moment and then began blinking in the order in which they'd been created. Reed began furiously typing and numbers and equations whizzed past on the monitor. The others watched in amazement as Reed's brilliant mind sifted through the numbers that appeared and disappeared before them.

Finally, Reed's face brightened. "It's the Catalan numbers sequence, modulo three-sixty."

General Hager spoke for them all when he said, "I don't follow you."

Reed began to explain. "The craters aren't random. They're appearing in numerical sequence."

"That means you can predict where the next one's going to be," Sue added.

Reed pulled out his PDA and began typing again. Captain Raye interrupted, holding out her cell phone. "Sir, I have them," she said, gesturing to the phone.

"Just a minute," General Hager told her.

Reed finished his computations. "Latitude: fifty-one degrees, twenty-five minutes north. Longitude: zero degrees, five minutes west."

Johnny's face fell—being an experienced pilot, he knew exactly where the Surfer would strike next.

Even General Hager sounded worried. "Well," he said quickly, "where is it?" His voice echoed in the silent room.

The inky night was punctuated by the small flicker of stars glowing dimly in the cold air. Beneath them, the Thames River moved slowly and silently, as dark as the night above. The military helicopter moved swiftly through the darkness, following the length of the murky river. The coordinates Reed had pinpointed as the location of the Surfer's next appearance had taken them all by surprise and added weight to an already heavy situation. Reed stared out the window of the helicopter and braced himself against the cold until he saw it.

The London Eye, also known as the Millennium Wheel, stood proudly against the river, its lights offering a balm to the darkness around it. The large observation wheel held thirty-two passenger capsules attached to its steel circumference and stretched over four hundred feet into the night sky. Shaped like a bicycle wheel, the London Eye rested on the western end of the Jubilee Gardens, on the south bank of the Thames. The impressive structure sat on the bank of the river, just near a pier that led to walkway down to the water. Even from the helicopter, Reed could see people riding inside the capsules, admiring the London skyline, or milling about in the gardens near the wheel or the adjacent County Hall. Quite an attraction in a heavily populated city. Reed shuddered to think what damage the Surfer would do.

General Hager seemed to be thinking the same thing. He looked over at Reed. "You sure your team can handle this alone?" he asked. "I'd feel better bringing in ground and air support."

"Trust me, General," Reed said. "This is what we do." Reed's confident words betrayed the apprehension he felt. They hadn't been battle-tested in a fight with the silver entity. Their previous encounter with it had almost destroyed the roof of the Baxter Building, and had left Johnny an unstable bundle of molecules. Reed feared what else could go wrong in an all-out battle with the Surfer.

General Hager eyed Reed, still looking skeptical. "Well, you're not going to be doing anything if you're wrong about the location."

Ben, who had kept his eyes on the view of the Thames from the helicopter, motioned downward and said, "I don't think you've got to worry about that."

They all peered below to see that the Thames was beginning to churn. A circle of water about the size of the Surfer's craters started to roil and froth, glowing with energy and light. The site of the sudden luminescence was silent except for the splashing of the water. People below crowded the banks of the Thames, astonished at the show of light, anticipating fireworks or more lights to add to the already impressive London skyline.

The military helicopter descended quickly and landed beside the Millennium Wheel, near the gardens. The sight of the copter landing caused more people to gather and stare. Inside the wheel's passenger cars, people could be seen angling for a better view of the skyline, the churning, glowing water, and the sudden arrival of military transport.

Reed and the others exited the copter quickly. He motioned to the crowd. "General, we need to clear these people out of here."

"I'm already on it, Richards," he said brusquely, as

soldiers began driving people away from the landing site and the perimeter surrounding the wheel, evacuating them from the area. "Don't tell me my job."

Reed ignored the general's comment and gathered his group. They stood directly behind the wheel, in the middle of the gardens, on a paved walkway lined with lighted trees. The wheel and the river stood directly in front of them. "If he surfaces soon, we've got to move the fight away from the crowds."

Johnny shook his head. "He's too fast for that. The second I see silver, I'm hitting him." Johnny started to walk toward the river.

"Wait," Reed yelled, careful not to touch him and trigger another shift of their powers. "You can't do that. We've got to stick to a plan and work as a team."

The last word seemed to catch Johnny's attention— and his ire. "Oh, we're still a team now? That's news to me."

Reed was taken aback. "What are you talking about?" he asked.

"You know," Johnny said, staring at his sister. Her face suddenly showed understanding.

"Johnny, this isn't really the time," she said.

Ben stepped forward and joined the fight. "The kid's got a point. You should have told us, Reed."

The Four started arguing, filling the normally quiet gardens with the sounds of their angry voices. Johnny made clear that he had overheard his sister's talk with

Reed and wasn't happy with their decision. The consequences of Johnny's fight with the Surfer hadn't aided his mental state, so he yelled. As did the others.

General Hager shoved his way into the middle of the argument to get their attention. "What the hell is wrong with you people?" he asked.

Before anyone in the group could respond, a loud *boom* sounded from the river. As one, they raced toward the Thames to witness the Silver Surfer bursting out of the glowing water. His high-velocity flight created a shock wave that hit the London Eye full force. The large steel wheel shook from the blast, the windows of the capsules shattering in bursts, jagged glass hitting the inhabitants and falling to the ground below. The structure's heavy frame began to wilt like wet paper, sending the entire thing tilting toward the river. The screams of those inside the capsules could be heard as they held on for dear life, their bodies bouncing against the metal and remaining glass like toys. One Japanese tourist fell hard against the rounded glass observation room, breaking the already cracked laminated glass and almost pitching out of the jagged window. He held on to the window frame, glass scratching his bloodied hands, his feet dangling in the cold night air as the wheel started to fall. His digital camera fell to the ground and shattered.

Suddenly the wheel stopped its descent, stuck at a forty-five-degree angle. Sue stood on the pier between the wheel and the river, her arms outstretched as she struggled to hold the seventeen-hundred-ton wheel up with a force field. Reed winced as he saw his fiancée's nose start to bleed with the strain. Then the wheel began to topple into the river; Sue's strength was waning.

"Ben, quickly!" Reed called out as he extended his arms into the cold night air, wrapping them around the metal wheel and weaving rapidly in and out of it steel spokes. Reed strained against the inertia of the substantial structure and held on to it while Ben tugged on the rest of his body, trying to anchor them all to the grounds of the Jubilee Gardens. Both Reed and the wheel screamed from the strain of their efforts, the cold metal eating into the flesh of his elongated form.

Johnny, having spied one man hanging out of a capsule, about to fall to his death, screamed "Hang on!" and took to the air, surrounded by his living flame. He was eager to get to the man in peril and didn't pay much attention to Reed's extended arms, which had been wrapped around several spokes of the wheel numerous times in his attempt to stabilize the shifting structure. Johnny reached out to grasp the hanging man, but his change in trajectory was too sudden for his speed and he brushed his arm against one of Reed's extended limbs.

Reed screamed "No!" as the direct contact with Johnny caused his body to retract, suddenly bathed in the powerful cosmic glow of Johnny's unstable molecular composition. Reed's entire body burst into flame as he absorbed Johnny's power, the side effect of the Human Torch's encounter with the Surfer once again wreaking havoc on the group. Ben, startled by the unexpected transformation, let go and Reed fell to the ground, setting the grass around him on fire.

Up in the air, a still glowing Johnny started to fall from the sky, his limbs stretching uselessly over the spokes of the wheel, where he was left dangling like many of the passengers in the capsules. And without the benefit of Reed anchoring it to the land inside the gardens, the wheel again began to tip.

The sudden, violent motion of the wheel tipping caused the Japanese tourist to finally lose his grip on the window frame. He shrieked as he realized he couldn't hold on and began falling toward the cold, hard ground. The air rushed all around him as he fell, and he began whispering prayers, anticipating his impact. But suddenly his fall was stopped, an invisible disc of energy catching him in midair and guiding him gently to the ground. He fell to his knees when he realized he was safely back on land, away from the shaking, rattling wheel.

Sue withdrew her force field once the man was safe and turned all her energy toward the wheel. The strain on her body was obvious to Reed as he watched her push her power to new limits. Sweat beaded on her forehead as she tried to hold on to the structure without the help of the others. The impact of the wheel caused Sue to lose ground as it literally pushed her away, shoving her back off the pier and over the water. She looked down at her feet, hovering above the water on an invisible disc of energy. Somehow, she kept her focus on both the wheel and the disc keeping her above the river. With the last ounce of her strength, Sue pushed her field against the wheel until it finally came to rest, upright. Reed watched Ben rush beneath it and brace it with his substantial frame, wrapping the ruined metal around itself and creating new beams of support. Sue floated back over to the pier, watching the water recede from her view. Once she made it to the pier, she collapsed.

Reed marveled at his fiancée's impressive display of power; he had never seen her like that. He had greatly underestimated the strength of her abilities. But his heart sank when he saw her collapse on the pier. "Sue!" he yelled and rushed over to her, leaving a set of flaming footprints behind him on the scorched grass. He spied one of Johnny's useless, elongated limbs dangling over a low part of the wheel and touched it, igniting the transformation between them once again.

Returned to his regular form, Reed again started for Sue. Johnny followed, but Reed turned to face him, keeping a safe distance. "Just stay back. You're going to get somebody killed!" Johnny stopped dead in his tracks, shaken by Reed's violent and dismissive tone.

Reed reached Sue's side just as she was regaining consciousness. He wiped some blood from her upper lip and cradled her head gently. He helped her get to her feet but stayed close as she tried to regain her strength and her footing. They looked back at the London Skyline, still intact beneath the black night sky. But something was different. In the light of the half-hidden moon, they saw that the once mighty Thames River was gone, completely drained in the aftermath of the Surfer's appearance. All that remained was a large silver crater resting at the bottom of the empty riverbed, its ethereal glow yet another reminder that time was running out to save the entire population of Earth.

A shudder ran through them both as they heard the wailing cry of an ambulance in the distance. It was then that Reed knew, deep in his heart, that they had failed.

11

THE EMBASSY OF THE UNITED STATES OF AMERICA was situated at the London Chancery Building in Grosvenor Square. The sprawling, rectangular building was nine stories high and dug three stories into the ground. A large gilded aluminum bald eagle with a wingspan of over thirty-five feet sat stoically on the roof of the chancery building, making it an instantly recognizable landmark in a city already crowded with stately architecture and breathtaking buildings. One of the largest United States diplomatic buildings in the world, its white facade and surrounding gardens gave the severe architecture an almost calm and peaceful aura.

Inside the building, it was an entirely different matter.

"What the hell was that?" General Hager's booming voice was more brusque than usual, and Reed couldn't blame him. The silver alien not only managed to escape their grasp but also dried up the Thames River, hurt numerous bystanders with its attack on the Millennium Wheel, and left a large crater in the middle of the now empty riverbed. According to Captain Raye, who'd spoken to them before Hager came into the room, the White House wasn't pleased, Downing Street wasn't pleased, and General Hager, the man responsible for the botched mission, was certainly not pleased.

Reed tried to console the irate general. "We'll make adjustments," he said. "Next time, we'll be ready." Despite his brave words, his confidence was shaken. Their second encounter with the Silver Surfer had been worse than the first. The strain of saving the wheel had pushed Sue to her limits and almost killed her. Johnny's unpredictability was greatly compounded by his unstable molecular structure, which caused him to switch powers with any member of the group he came into physical contact with. And Ben? His strength was matched only by the intensity of the cold shoulder he was currently giving Reed. Reed hated to admit it, but he knew this wasn't the Fantastic Four's finest hour.

Hager's gruff voice interrupted his thoughts. "Next time?! There *is* no next time. You can't handle this alone. That's why I brought in some help." He motioned to a guard, who left the room.

Reed began to protest. "General, bringing in more soldiers and weaponry is only going to put innocent people in danger."

A disembodied voice answered Reed's statement. "More than *you* already have?"

The source of the voice was unmistakable. After all, each of the Four had heard it, at some point, in their nightmares. Since the cosmic storm. Since the attempts on their lives. Since the fight that left him dead, burned and frozen in his own metallic skin.

Reed and the others turned in the direction of the voice and were stunned into silence. Standing in front of them, alive and able, was Victor Von Doom, back from the dead. Only Reed, after a few moments, managed to find his voice: "Victor?"

"What's the matter?" Victor asked, a smile twisting his mangled, damaged face. "Afraid of ghosts?"

The shocked inaction of the Fantastic Four lasted only a moment. They sprung into motion, once again ready to face their sworn enemy. Johnny clenched his fists and turned them to flame, ready to hurl fireballs at the man who had once tried to kill almost everyone in the room. Ben acted more boldly, leaping toward Victor. He threw Von Doom hard against the wall, his massive hand clutching Victor's silver throat.

"If you're a ghost," Ben said through clenched teeth, "then you won't mind if I break your scrawny neck." Ben tightened his grip on Victor. Reed gave a momentary shudder as he recalled the severity of their last battle. They had torn through several buildings and an entire block in Manhattan before bringing him down.

General Hager's voice rang out across the room. "Let him go!"

"Do you know who this is?" Johnny asked incredulously.

Hager looked at Johnny and said, "He's Victor Von Doom, and he is here on my orders. Guards!"

A dozen heavy machine guns were suddenly cocked and pointed squarely at Ben. The thick, metal-tipped bullets might not pierce Ben's hide, but Reed didn't want to take that chance. "Ben," Reed said calmly. "Let him go."

Reed could see the thought processes running through Ben's rocky head. Everything in Ben wanted to squash Victor's neck like a grape. But slowly, digit by digit, he released his grip on Von Doom. Victor collapsed to the floor, coughing and gasping for breath.

Reed walked over to his former classmate, who looked terrible. But he was alive. "How is this possible?" Reed asked, his voice low and dark. "How can you be alive?"

Victor stood up, brushing dust from his coat. "No thanks to you four, that's for certain." Victor's eyes wandered across the room until they fell on Sue. She returned his gaze, no doubt as shocked to see him alive as they all were, before Johnny closed in next to her in a protective gesture.

General Hager walked over to Victor as if asserting his own protective stance. "Victor Von Doom has made contact with the alien. He's got valuable information."

Victor nodded his head. "Information that might just save the planet," he said in a mockingly heroic

141

voice. He made eye contact with Sue once again, but she looked away, disgusted at the sight of him despite the fact that there was a time when Victor would have given her the world.

Victor turned back to the group. "Now let's be clear about this. I hate you. *All* of you. But the world's at stake. We need to work together to survive."

Reed was not oblivious to Victor's longing glances at Sue. The mere fact that Victor was alive triggered a plethora of feelings within him, feelings he'd rather leave buried. "General," he said, "we know firsthand that if you trust Victor, you're going to regret it."

General Hager looked Reed squarely in the eye so there would be no confusion. "So far the only one I've regretted trusting here is *you*, Richards." He spit Reed's name out like a curse.

Reed met the general's hard gaze with equal fervor. The fact that Reed was flexible didn't mean he was weak. He was getting more than tired of answering to the barking general, who constantly seemed to need Reed's help and to hate him for it. As he considered all his options, Reed exchanged looks with Sue. She was still a bit weak from their battle at the river, and that might account for her silence. Victor's reappearance surely didn't help. He wanted to tell her once again that it was right thing to do, for them to leave the Four—and a normal life was sounding pretty good to him right then.

Those thoughts were pushed out of his head by Ben's deep voice saying, "Reed, don't agree to this." But this crisis was larger than any feud between rivals, any sparks from flashing egos. Life on Earth was in peril. Finding and stopping the Surfer had to be their first priority. Everything else, once again, would have to wait.

"Let's see what he's got." Reed said finally. He didn't have to look at Ben, he could feel the waves of disappointment coming from him.

Victor walked over to a large flat-screen monitor near a computer set into the wall. He loaded a small silver disc into the machine while the rest of the group looked on in silence. The only sound in the room was the mechanical *whir* and *click* of the computer loading Victor's data. "I made a detailed recording of my little encounter with him," Victor said, pulling up the information onto the large screen in front of them, which began playing a video of Victor's meeting with the Surfer. The four watched intently as Victor fought with the alien, unleashing his powerful torrents of electricity upon the silver entity to no effect.

Reed made special note of the fact that Victor still appeared as powerful as ever. His time missing in action hadn't quelled any of his extraordinary abilities; Victor could still manipulate electricity to his whim. Reed tried to sound uninterested when he asked, "How did you find him?"

A wry smile spread over Victor's wrecked face. "Catalan number system. I'm surprised it took you so long to figure out." Victor turned back to the video playing on the computer screen and froze the action the moment after the Surfer blasted him. "Well?"

Ben was the first to speak up. "I liked the part when he knocked you on your ass."

Victor dismissed Ben with a wave of his hand. He motioned to the bottom of the computer screen, where a graphic monitored and measured the expenditure of energy. "Look where the energy levels surge when he attacks me. We see a peak in his board." Victor ran the video again slowly, keeping a close eye on the measuring instrument. It suddenly spiked in number and intensity. "There," Victor said. "You see what happened?"

Reed was catching on, his eyes glued to the screen. "The energy was channeled through him, but it originated from the board."

Sue stepped closer to the monitor, trying to keep a safe distance from Victor. "So his board isn't just a means of transportation for him. It's actually the source of his power."

Victor nodded. "If we could separate him from it, we could cut off his power completely."

"Then that's what we have to do." General Hager stared hard at Victor, feeling his faith was well placed.

"How?" Johnny asked.

Victor looked at the young man. "If I knew that," he said dismissively, "I wouldn't need you people, would I?"

Reed ignored Victor's tone, instead focusing his attention on the computer screen. His mind was already racing in many different directions, thinking of possible scenarios and formulas that might be useful to them. Reed was sure that separating the Surfer from his power source was the key to defeating him. "It's almost like he has a symbiotic relationship with it. We need to find out exactly what that link is so we can break it."

General Hager had apparently heard enough. "You two should get to work," he barked. Hager barely looked at the others as he left the room.

Victor walked over to Reed, placing his hand firmly on Reed's shoulder. Reed chilled at the metallic touch. "I'm so glad we have this chance to collaborate again," Victor said coolly. "I'll try to talk slowly so you can keep up."

Ben Grimm walked slowly through the damp streets of London with Johnny hot on his tail. Their encounter with the Surfer, and now with Victor, weighed heavily on his mind. Ben himself was growing increasingly concerned about the future not only of the group but of the entire planet. Ben couldn't even get close to the Surfer, and he had barely been able to hold up the wheel as it was tipping over. He hadn't felt so useless in a fight in a very long time. And he didn't like it. He couldn't even put his hands on Victor without it turning into a government incident.

He ignored Johnny and pulled his overcoat higher toward his face, trying to conceal his appearance as he wandered the unfamiliar London streets. Passersby cut him a wide berth, as they usually did, and he missed the more familiar streets of New York City. But he ignored them, too, since he was on the hunt. *One on every corner,* Alicia had told him. He intended to prove her right.

Just as Ben rounded the corner a few blocks away from the embassy, he found his mark. The Red Rock Pub sat stately and quiet, nestled into the corner building on a cobblestone street. The bay windows were trimmed in white. He noticed a rocky cliff painted on the door as he walked into the pub with Johnny right behind him. Ben strode up the bar and put one meaty hand down on the counter. The quaint, dimly lit bar suited his mood perfectly. He needed some quiet as much as he needed a drink.

A few rounds later, Ben was feeling better. The pub was becoming increasingly filled with people and noise. Johnny had managed to pull him away from the bar to a corner table near a dartboard. Johnny kept throwing darts between sentences, as if they emphasized his points.

"How can we be working on the same side as Victor?" he asked for the third time.

Ben took a long pull from his pitcher of beer. "You got me, pal. Things were a lot simpler when I could just whale on the guy."

Johnny drew back to throw another dart, but his anger got the better of him and his fingers ignited, sending the flaming dart right into the center of the board. The entire dartboard soon caught fire. Several nearby patrons turned to look at the small blaze suspended on the wall.

Johnny ran to the board and dumped his pint of lager over it, extinguishing the flames. "Sorry," he said to the owner of the pub, who was suddenly standing by his side, staring at the ruined board. "I'll pay for that." The owner turned away in a huff.

Johnny walked back over to Ben, who continued to sit slouched over his drink. "We wouldn't even be in this position if I wasn't such a complete screw-up," Johnny said, picking up a fresh pint of lager.

Ben looked over at Johnny, who had taken a seat at the table. "Hey, you're not a complete screw-up. A *partial* screw-up, maybe."

"Thanks," Johnny said weakly.

Ben finished the rest of his pitcher in one long gulp. "Look, there's nothing you or me can do now. It's all up to the eggheads."

A serious look suddenly crossed Johnny's face. "You

think Reed's right?" he asked Ben. "That this might really be the end of the world?"

Ben nodded his head. "He's never wrong about stuff like this."

A silence fell between them as they contemplated the idea that the end might be at hand. Ben had always tried not to think about such a thing, even in the thick of a battle.

"You know," Johnny began, "I'm not a very deep kinda guy . . ."

"No?" Ben asked, mocking Johnny's attempt at a sincere tone.

"I'm just saying," Johnny continued, lowering his voice, "if we can't stop this, if it's really the end of the world . . . how are you going to spend your last few minutes?"

The question hung in the air between them. Ben stared into his empty pitcher and thought about it. "Part of me would like to go out fighting," he said finally, resting his rocky hand on the table. "But to tell you the truth, I think I'd like to spend my last few minutes holding on to Alicia."

"That sounds good to me," Johnny said absentmindedly, at first not noticing Ben's jealous glare. When he realized what he'd said, Johnny tried to backtrack. "Not holding on to Alicia, because she's your girlfriend, not mine," he stammered. "I have no interest in her whatsoever," he added, but Ben's look was getting worse. "Not that she's not attractive, because she is. *So* attractive. I mean, who wouldn't want to . . ." Johnny watched the glass pitcher shatter in Ben's hand. The table started to tip and groan. "Actually," Johnny offered, "going out fighting. That's what I'd want to do." He exhaled heavily.

Ben still eyed him warily. "Oh, you'll go out fighting," he said. But in his gut, Ben knew the kid had a point. He doubted any of them would be of much use in a fight. The Surfer was too strong, too mysterious. And too powerful. Deep inside, Ben Grimm knew that they were in for the fight of their lives. And unless Reed came up with something soon, Ben knew it was a fight the Fantastic Four were bound to lose.

12

THEIR SUBSEQUENT DAYS IN LONDON WERE MUCH LIKE the first: gray skies, drizzling rain, and an overwhelming silence over the entire embassy. Susan Storm walked the halls of the building, its dark paneled walls leading her in circles. She watched the officious staff go about their duties in silence, shuffling papers, not talking above a whisper, as if they, too, understood the dire implications of the events of the last few days. The disappearance of the Thames had taken a toll on everyone here, most of them native Brits, and the loss of such a public gathering place was a huge blow to their morale. Sue gathered from their vacant stares and lack of eye contact that they knew things were bad. She wondered if they blamed her for their loss, even though she had practically killed herself saving the people on the Millennium Wheel. It still stood, albeit with newly welded supports in place near its base, a jarring and ugly reminder of the losing battle the Four had fought there.

Sue couldn't blame the staff for their sad demeanor. She, too, felt the heaviness all around the embassy, and the weather didn't help. She watched her brother skulk off into corners, afraid of getting too close to anyone in the group. He stayed close only to Ben—they often did that after a particularly difficult fight. Neither would admit it, but she knew that the two very different personalities found comfort in each other after a battle. Reed was sealed off in a lab with Victor, looking for a way to sever the Surfer from his power source. All she was left to do was keep to herself, out of everyone's way, nursing her headaches with paracetamol, walking the endless halls of the embassy, waiting. Waiting for better news.

She rounded the corner of another hallway, this one more familiar because it was near the temporary lab that had been set up for Reed and Victor. She couldn't help the dark thoughts that formed in her head like a coming storm when she thought about Victor working with them again. *Nothing good can come from this*, she told herself again and again. And yet, as much as she hated to admit it, Reed needed help. If they were to have any chance of defeating the Surfer and saving the planet, they would have to pool all their available resources. And right now, Victor was one of those resources.

She walked quietly into the lab, hoping not to disturb Reed. She found him hunched over his PDA, typing madly at the device. Something about the familiar scene touched her; how many times had she walked into his lab at the Baxter Building and seen the very same thing? Even here in this place far from home, Reed was still the same man he always was. The man she loved.

Just then, Reed slammed his fist on the table and threw the PDA across the room. Such outbursts from him were rare, usually occurring only when he was unnecessarily provoked or extremely frustrated. The durable adamantium case saved the PDA from shattering against the floor, but the loud crash echoed in the otherwise silent room. Sue ran to his side, placing her arms on his shoulders.

"I can't find the link," he said. His voice was defeated and low.

"Shh . . ." she said, rubbing his shoulders, feeling the tense muscles beneath his uniform. He always tied himself in knots, she knew, both literally and figuratively. She tried to bring him some comfort by rubbing the stiff tendons in his neck. "Just relax," she said, in a voice calm and soft. "Clear your mind. Breathe in deeply. Feel yourself letting go. All the way from your head to your feet."

Sue could feel Reed loosen under her firm grip, his shoulders waving like liquid beneath his suit, his right arm extending and collecting like a puddle on the floor. Reed slid down lower in his chair, his body stretching and softening. Sue came closer to him, bringing her lips to his neck, caressing his skin with her breath. "Relax," she said in a whisper. She went to kiss him. "Feel your pulse slowing down . . ."

Suddenly Reed's body became as rigid as steel. He froze, leaving Sue in the middle of a now one-sided kiss. "A pulse," he said.

"What?" Sue asked.

"A *tachyon* pulse!" Reed exclaimed, stretching his hand to the corner of the room and retrieving his PDA. "Thank you!" He grabbed her quickly, planting a swift kiss on her lips. Then he went back to his furious typing.

"Glad I could be of help," she said, crossing her arms and watching him retreat into his work once again. She stayed for a moment longer before quietly leaving the room.

The next few days found Reed—and sometimes Victor—furiously implementing the new plan. Blueprints and schematics lay strewn across the floor of the lab as special metal posts were welded together. Four small satellite dishes were brought into the lab and left in the corner, near where Victor stood. Victor stayed quiet, watching Reed work. He had seen the blueprints and, secretly, he was impressed. Reed had done it. *So it seems*, Victor thought, *that I'm not the only one with a plan*. His eyes burned with envy as he watched Reed construct the new device. Victor pitched in when he had to, boosting the electrical dexterity of the device where Reed asked him to, helping him place the heavy and awkward components where they needed to be. All the while Sue assisted her fiancé, avoiding Victor's increasingly rabid stares, focused solely on one task: saving the planet from the clutches of the Silver Surfer.

When they were done, Reed summoned the others and some of the military personnel into the laboratory.

General Hager entered the lab without his usual entourage. He looked around the room for his aide, Captain Raye, and noticed her absence. Sue's brother also was absent, which seemed to further sour the general's already-gruff demeanor.

Victor allowed Reed to take center stage, at which Reed proceeded with an explanation for the strange equipment all around them—equipment that Victor was sure Hager's mind could never comprehend. Inevitably, the general felt the need to interrupt. "Just what the hell is a tachyon pulse?"

Reed slowed down, attempting to translate the complex science behind the device into lay terms. "It's a stream of subatomic particles that move faster than light," he explained.

"It's the link between the Surfer and his board," Sue added.

Ben Grimm leaned in closer, examining one of the

complex portable devices. "These things Reed's building can jam the signal."

Victor saw that the general still looked perplexed. Reed, ever the optimist, grabbed his PDA and punched in a few commands. Suddenly, a holographic projection rose above it, displaying a jamming field connected by four separate points. The projection showed how the four points could create a field of energy, the output of which would sever the link between the Surfer and his board.

The general's eyes lit up. "Like catching fish in a net," he said. He looked over at Victor, who ignored him.

"Exactly," Reed said. "When we activate the field, it'll separate him from his board, making him powerless. In theory, anyway."

The general, unsurprisingly, ignored Reed's disclaimer. "How long before it's operational?" Hager asked.

"Three hours," Reed responded.

With that, Victor left the crowded laboratory. *Soon*, he thought. Better to let Reed and the others implement their plan. For now. There would be still be enough time for Victor to implement a plan of his own.

A few doors down from the lab, near the Fantastic Four's quarters, Captain Raye was lost in thought.

She had been reviewing the data on the Surfer, looking for new ways to approach the problem. Nothing in her training had prepared her for this, and yet still she pushed herself. Too little sleep and too much fear had nearly paralyzed her. The feeling of fear went against everything she had been trained to do: Find the problem, conquer the problem, eliminate the problem. Her dreams were haunted by thoughts of the coming apocalypse, nightmares where her body was slowly covered in a shiny silver alloy, leaving her unable to breathe and drying her up like the Thames River. She'd awake covered in sweat and wrapped in clammy sheets, her skin once again returned to its pale pallor, her eyes swollen and rimmed with redness.

She told herself to control it, to forget her fear and focus on solving the problem at hand. She told herself she had been spending too much time in the presence of odd characters: the video of the silver entity, the strange powers of the Fantastic Four, the creepy and metallic Victor Von Doom. She needed to be around normal people. She was tired of the company of these strangers.

She turned a corner, lot in her thoughts, and ran straight into Johnny Storm. She looked up to see the young man covered only by a white towel, wet from a shower in the nearby bathroom. She fought to control her eyes as they traveled over his trim and muscular physique. *He can really fill out that uniform*, one of her girlfriends had whispered suggestively to her. Raye had to admit that her friend was not wrong.

She cleared her throat and tried to sound official. Off-putting, even. "Mr. Storm, we're heading to intercept the Surfer in ten minutes, with you or without you." She kept her eyes locked on his, fighting the temptation to steal another glance at his body.

Johnny picked up on her forced seriousness and smiled. "You sure you didn't just come here to see me in a towel?" He fumbled with his grip on the fabric around his waist, pretending it was about to fall. *Pathetic*, Raye thought, her face remaining passive and uninterested. Then she felt a blast of warmth, and the water clinging to Johnny's exposed body started to dance and sizzle as he steamed himself dry.

Captain Raye made a disgusted noise in the back of her throat and attempted to walk by.

Johnny stepped in front of her. "Hey, why are you so down on me?" he asked. "You don't even know me."

Adjusting the papers in her hand, Captain Raye addressed him directly. "Actually, I know you very well. I read your classified personality profile. Jonathan Spencer Storm. Confident, highly competitive, unafraid to take risks."

A big grin broke out on Johnny's face. "Sounds right," he said, stepping closer to her.

Raye continued in her matter-of-fact tone. "Reckless, irresponsible. Self-obsessed, bordering on narcissism. Involved in a long series of superficial romantic liaisons, indicating an inability to form lasting, meaningful relationships."

"I sometimes cry during chick flicks. Was that in there?" She scowled at him. "Look," Johnny continued, "there's more to me than just that. I swear. I just want to get to know you while there's still time." He tried using his very best puppy-dog face on her, but she was undeterred. She simply walked past him.

Johnny followed. "C'mon, Captain. At least tell me your first name," he pleaded. Captain Raye remained silent and continued walking away from him. Johnny reached out to grab her shoulder. Before he knew what was happening, Captain Raye grabbed his wrist and threw him over her shoulder in a swift and classic judo move. Johnny landed flat on his back on the hard floor of the embassy, barely managing to keep his towel secure. His gaze rose up to meet her face, which was looking squarely down on him from above. "I've never been more in love with anyone than I am at this second."

Captain Raye's serious facade collapsed like a crumbling wall of bricks. She grinned in spite of herself, staring down at the half-naked man in front of her. She let out a small laugh. "The name's Frankie," she said. "Now get up and get your clothes on."

She walked past the fallen hero, who still sat dumbfounded on the floor, and she could feel him watching her leave, his gaze as palpable on her body as an overcoat. She increased her pace until she was safely down the hall and out of his sight. Shaking her head, she reprimanded herself for being so easily swayed by his charm. *You need more sleep*, she told herself. *That, and find some normal people to hang around. That is, if there's still a world tomorrow.*

13

EVEN THE NAME SEEMED PRIMITIVE AND SINISTER: the Black Forest, nestled deep in the German countryside in the southwest corner of the state of Baden-Württemberg, not far from the more modern and graceful Baden-Baden. It was a crowded sea of pine trees and mountains, secluded in its forestry and peppered with villages and small cottages more than three hundred years old. The dense forest made the landscape seem otherworldly, cast deep in its shadows, hidden from the modern world. The land held a rich, ancient mythology. Stories had been passed down for generations about the werewolves and witches that haunted the dark woods, living among the thick trees, scratching their names into the ruddy trunks.

Yet for all the mysterious creatures that supposedly inhabited these woods, none were as powerful as the silver alien walking through them now. The bright morning light barely penetrated the sheath of trees as the Surfer made his way through the forest, oblivious to the austere and awesome sight of the ancient growth around him. He listened intently to a sound coming deep from the living Earth, following its mysterious song until he had passed through a copse of trees into a flat, shadowed clearing. The area was darker here, in one of the most remote sections of the forest. He closed his eyes for a moment, lost to the song, and raised his hands. The air surrounding his hands began to move, the molecules trembling in his presence, as a strong wind began to stir around him. The blowing wind began to glow, silver specks of dust becoming radiant, small stars in a cosmic cloud that began to pulse and grow. Everything the cloud touched wilted and shuddered, the leaves browning in an instant, the trees bowing and shriveling as if acknowledging their defeat at the hands by something older and stronger than they were.

The surrounding forest and muddy floor seemed to fall away as the Surfer began to bore deep into the time-less soil, hollowing it out, destroying every living thing in his path. Replacing the living greens and browns with his silver hue, remaking the world in his own likeness.

His actions did not go unnoticed. A few miles away, a new, more modern village had been erected. United States military-issue green tents were already in place, housing centers for communications, combat, and sur-veillance. Squads of soldiers stood nearby, armed to the teeth with the latest in heavy artillery. Empty crates of guns and ammo were cast aside as useless timber. The guards stood as sentinels outside the tent of General Hager, alert in mind and body, waiting to receive their orders to move out.

Inside the tent, the general and his associates monitored the Surfer on sophisticated radar equipment, enhanced by Reed's radiation sensors. The air inside the tent was as thick as the surrounding forest, and each member of the team was on heightened alert, ready to do what he must to save the planet. Each person in the tent had experienced the awesome power of their foe, and knew the consequences should they not be able to defeat him. Reed monitored his equipment as best he could, keeping one eye on the signal given off by the Surfer. *You're not getting away this time*, he thought.

Captain Raye looked up from her viewing screen, the green light casting shadows on her angular face. "He's holding his position north of here." Her voice was even and calm, covering the anxiety that was lodged in her gut.

"Good," General Hager said. He was poring over combat strategies and weapon lists, ignoring the others in the tent. Reed approached him, ready to take the lead.

"General, give us a one-mile perimeter," he said, nodding to Ben. Sue and Johnny gathered near, ready to begin their attack.

"Forget it," General Hager answered, getting in

Reed's face, causing him to stumble back a step or two. "You had your chance, and you blew it. This is a military operation. You jam the signal and then get out of the way. We'll handle the rest." He turned dismissively away from Reed and went back to his paperwork, surrounded by his minions in their Kevlar vests and other combat gear.

Reed was taken aback by the general's outburst. It was a bit much, even for the gruff commander. "You don't understand . . ." Reed began.

General Hager turned to Reed, fire shining in the whites of his eyes. His raised voice filled the entire tent. "No, *you* don't understand, so let me make it clear for you and your pack of freaks here. I am the quarterback. You are on *my* team. Got it?" Reed shrunk a little at the tone and volume of the general's voice. Aside from Ben, they all did. But the general wasn't finished. In a tone dripping with snide condescension, Hager added, "I guess you didn't play a lot of football back in high school, did you, Richards?"

The tent fell silent in the aftermath of General Hager's childish insult.

Reed felt a strong emotion rising inside of him. It all finally caught up with him: the stress and frustration of fighting an elusive opponent like the Surfer, the endless nights without sleep, the tension brewing within his own group over his decision to leave the Four with Sue—not to mention the irascibility of an increasingly arrogant blowhard like General Hager. This plan wouldn't exist without Reed or his great intellect; Victor had done very little to help with the creation of the jamming device. It was all on Reed's shoulders, just as it always had been: the future of the Four, the future of his life with Sue, and now the future of the planet. Mr. Fantastic was fed up. And Hager was starting a high-school pissing contest?

Reed's voice was strong and clear when he finally spoke. "You're right, General. I didn't play sports. I stayed inside and studied like a good little *nerd*." In his growing anger, he emphasized the last word. "And now, fifteen years later, I am one of the greatest minds of the twenty-first century and I am engaged to the hottest girl on the planet. And the big jock who played quarterback in high school? He's standing right in front of me, asking me for *my* help. And I say he's not going to get a damn thing if he doesn't do exactly what I tell him to and start treating my friends and me with some respect."

Reed's usually flexible body was rigid with anger and his hands shook with fury. His eyes bored into Hager as the general's had so often bored into him. Somewhere within himself Reed knew that there was no time for this, no time for a fight of egos with enough sparks to burn down the immense forest around them. Maybe it was the landscape, the deep, brooding forest imbuing them with an almost prehistoric sense of battle and hierarchy. But there could be only one leader. A line had been drawn. Reed had snapped, and there was no going back.

The face of General Hager remained solid and unmoving, like the trees around them. His eyes betrayed no emotion, nor did his erect posture falter. The only part of his body that moved was his mouth, as his lips parted to speak. "Give him what he wants."

The general left the tent with Victor following him.

The rest of the officers continued with their duties, monitoring the Surfer and the presence of the new crater. The Four gathered once again around Reed, their undisputed leader. Sue leaned into her fiancé and whispered into his ear: "I am *so* hot for you right now."

Johnny embraced Reed from behind in a mocking, brotherly hug. "Me too!" he cheered.

Reed smiled, but only for a moment. They had a job to do.

The deep forest seemed endless and swallowed the Fantastic Four entirely. Daylight could be seen gracing only the tops of the trees; the carpet of the forest was cool and clammy under their feet. What struck Reed first was how intensely silent it was; no sound existed outside of the small twitter of their own movements through the brush. Each member of the Four carried a small metal container the size of a suitcase. The hard, silver metal barely let off a glare, having little sunlight to reflect. Reed was going through the calculations in his mind once again, looking for any holes in his theory. He could find none. It was up to them now, each member of the team ready to perform the task that would help them take the Surfer down.

Reed once again consulted a small GPS device in his hand. "All right," he said. "This is it. Set up your post then rendezvous back here."

Each of the Four carried a similar GPS device. They exchanged a quick look and then went off—four cases, four members, four separate directions.

Reed watched the others leave, silently wishing them all luck. His gaze lingered the longest on Sue, as he watched her disappear into a thicket of trees. She was soon lost to him, invisible in the density of the forest. He once again consulted his GPS device and made his own way to the designated location.

The cool air of the forest followed Reed closely as he darted through trees and brush. The shadows of the trees fell far, appearing to stretch and lengthen on the forest floor. Reed reached his point, near two large tree stumps, and set the metal case on the ground with a delicate thud. He hit a keypad on the side of the case and stepped back to let the machine activate. Legs emerged from the bottom of the case, raising it above the floor of the forest. The top of the case opened silently, allowing a small transmitter to rise into the air above it. The entire device was not unlike a large tripod, with a pulse emitter on top instead of a camera. A blinking light at the top of the post let Reed know his device was operational. It was ready.

Elsewhere in the expansive forest, Johnny followed the readings on his GPS and soon reached his own destination. He felt a shiver travel up his spine, and he marveled at how a forest so thick with heavy pine trees could inspire in him such feelings of isolation. He shook the thoughts away and punched the keypad on the side of his device. He watched it spring to life and then stood by, waiting.

Meanwhile, Ben Grimm crunched his way through the brush in another part of the forest, squeezing his way through the trees. He stopped to scratch his back against the side of a thick trunk, rubbing himself as the leaves fell around him. His GPS device started beeping, signaling that he had reached his destination. He set the case down and used a thin branch he found on the ground to trigger the keypad. He looked up to see a large bear nearby, scratching its own back on a tree a few feet away. The bear paused, making eye contact with Ben. "What do you want?" Ben asked.

Just then, Ben heard Reed's voice come through the com link on his wrist. "What's our status?" Reed asked him.

"I'm good to go," Ben replied, noticing that the bear had disappeared.

Johnny's voice soon came through on the line. "Same here."

Sue heard her friends' voices coming through her com link as she struggled through a twisted copse of trees. She reached a dark clearing in the woods filled with underbrush and fallen trunks. It was noticeably cooler in the shadowed clearing than it had been just a few moments ago, and she smirked at her luck, having landed in the coldest and most barren part of the woods. *The Black Forest indeed,* she thought as she set down her case.

She heard Reed's voice call her name over the com link. "Almost there," she replied, triggering the keypad on the side of her metal case.

Just then she heard a rustling behind her. She felt heat on her back as the darkness around her became illuminated by an ominous, silver glow. Suddenly, the massive trees wiggled and bent, warping unnaturally to create an opening. She felt her heart start beating faster. "Guys," she said softly. "We may have a problem."

She had barely heard Reed asking "What's wrong?" when she saw it. The Silver Surfer, luminescent in the dark woods, flew through the clearing, causing the leaves to rustle and the trees to shake and wither.

"He's here," she said. Her voice held a tremor of fear.

Reed's urgent voice flew out of the com link. "Get out of there now!"

Sue turned back to the metal case. She hadn't activated the keypad. "It's not set up yet," she said into her com link.

Reed's reply was immediate: "Forget about it! Just get out of there!"

But Sue could not hear him. She stood transfixed, unable to turn away from the glowing figure before her. It was the first time she had seen the entity up close. The surrounding woods were bathed in the Surfer's glow. This time, the light gently caressed the trees, warming their trunks with its radiance. The chill in the air departed and Sue felt deep inside of her a sense of everything growing, everything breathing, alive. Her hands fell listlessly to her sides, the com link crackling and going dead in the radiation put off by the glowing silver entity.

The Silver Surfer stood atop his thin, elegant board, a few feet from Sue and the metal case. He looked resplendent as he hovered there in the warm air. She could see his powerful legs humming with energy and his arms gracefully suspended, gliding atop air currents she could not see. She could feel her face turn warmer, and as she basked in the Surfer's presence she suddenly had a sense of how every living thing was made of energy, how everything felt connected. The roots in the soil, the unseen insects carefully trawling through the trees and brush, the endless streaming light that was now all around her. She took in a deep breath of air and that, too, was alive, filled with molecules and motes of life-sustaining oxygen. Even the trees seemed to breathe, contributing to the swirling, thriving system all around her. It was almost euphoric; her limbs trembled and her mind danced. She understood that everything in the world held its purpose, connected by one and the same.

She did not flinch as the Surfer lowered himself on his board, meeting her unblinking gaze. She noticed that his face was calm and smooth, his eyes filled with light. It was the most gentle and radiant visage she had ever encountered and deep inside she felt no fear, no hesitation. She felt only comfort and companionship, as if all her aching questions about the world around her were suddenly and finally being answered. She did not fight the small smile that grew on her warm face, and as if by instinct she reached out to touch the celestial being in front of her.

The Surfer silently returned her gaze; the connection was not one-sided. The same hand that had doomed planets reached out into the infinite space between the Surfer and Susan Storm. He reached out into that abyss and touched her cheek.

Sue leaned into the gentle, caressing touch. Her cheek flushed, bathed in his radiance. Unafraid, she looked into his face, his eyes like two deep pools of liquid silver. She held his gaze and asked, "Why are you destroying our world?"

The Surfer appeared startled, genuinely surprised by the directness of her question.

"If you are going to do it," she continued softly, "we at least have the right to know why."

The Surfer furrowed his silver brow as if contemplating his actions for the first time. Sue saw his face turn sad, a bit of darkness tarnishing the silver luster of his skin. His voice, deep and trembling, matched hers in its softness: "I have no choice."

It was then that Sue saw it, just underneath the radiant glow in his eyes. His gentle face did not hold the hunger for power she had so often seen in Victor's face, nor did it hold the posturing and authority she had seen in the gruff scowl of General Hager. The Surfer's face held only aching regret and contrition. She could suddenly feel the sadness overcome every inch of her body.

Before she could reply, Sue heard a crashing in the woods behind her. She heard Reed's voice echo across the clearing: "Get back!"

She turned to face him, her arms no longer listless but held out before her. "Wait," she said, watching as Ben and Johnny also reached the clearing. They were surrounded. The air around them once again turned charged and aggressive. "Wait."

Sue turned back to the Surfer. His eyes were tentative, suddenly fearful at the arrival of the others, at the radical change in their environment. She tried to calm him using an even tone. "What do you mean you have no choice? There's always a choice."

The Surfer looked heartbroken when he met her eyes, his ethereal voice catching in his throat. "Not always."

Yards away, General Hager's hands shook with anger as he watched through binoculars the Four in front of the silver alien, just standing there. *Are they talking to it?* he thought, flabbergasted. "What the hell is going on there?" he said under his breath. "C'mon, Richards, just jam the damn signal!" He couldn't let another chance to kill this alien slip away from them. He was the leader responsible for this mission. Combat decisions were his alone to make. He lowered the binoculars in disgust.

He turned to see Victor standing next to him, holding a missile launcher. "Maybe he could use a little persuasion," Victor said, his voice low and deep.

Sue remained adamant, keeping the Surfer locked in her gaze. He was growing more skittish as Ben, Reed, and Johnny inched closer to them. His glow had receded and the air around them once again felt cold. But Sue couldn't let him go. Not yet. "Why do you want to destroy our world?" she asked again.

The Surfer looked confused, then almost childlike. "I am not the destroyer."

"Then who is?" Reed asked, keeping his eyes on Sue, his heart in his throat as he inched closer.

The Surfer's mouth opened slightly, hesitantly, as if he were afraid to answer. He looked at Sue with a face tinged with sorrow, as if he knew the answer would cause her pain. Just then, a high-pitched whine coursed through the air. The group turned to see a barrage of heavily armed missiles heading right toward the Silver Surfer. And Sue.

The Surfer immediately grabbed Sue and pulled her behind him, moving to the other side of a ridge of trees. Assured that she was out of the line of fire, the Surfer sped off toward the incoming barrage of flying missiles. He raised his hand and turned the weapons to ash. They crumbled, carried harmlessly away on the cool wind of the forest.

General Hager could not believe his eyes. Through the gaze of the binoculars, he watched the Surfer dismantle and destroy their most sophisticated land-to-air missiles. The floor seemed to give way, and his stomach dropped when he saw the Surfer heading directly toward him. "Open fire!" he yelled, releasing the flood of weaponry at his disposal.

Suddenly General Hager was surrounded by his troops, who unleashed their ammunition at the glowing silver being. Bullets, grenades, concussion blasts, even flares. Nothing touched the alien. The Surfer reached the military space and flew overhead, raising his hands. With his simple gesture, all the guns and launchers burst into flames. Soldiers watched their gear explode in their hands, sending flames up their arms and into the air. Medics scrambled to put out the fires on the fallen soldiers while others dropped of their own accord and rolled around in the dirt in an attempt to extinguish the flames. The air held a distinct smell of ash.

Hager and Victor dove into the brush for cover as the Surfer flew back, his board parting the air just above their heads. The Surfer continued back to the clearing where the Fantastic Four still stood.

Reed could hear the explosions and screaming coming from Hager's command post. It didn't take much imagination to know the Surfer had eliminated the threat to himself. Reed was eager to learn more about what the Surfer could tell them, but Hager's aggressive act had ruined all attempts at diplomacy. The Surfer was too powerful to be left to his own devices; Reed needed to disarm him.

He reached down to his PDA, which was linked to all four metal cases. He punched in the command to activate the posts but the controls only flashed the word ERROR. Something had gone wrong. "It's not yet working. The last post isn't set up," he yelled.

Sue sprung into action. "I'm on it!" she yelled.

She raced back to her metal case and activated the keypad. She watched the legs sprout out, but the transmitter did not rise from the top of the case.

In the meantime, Johnny and Ben had gathered around Reed. The Surfer flew around the clearing and hovered, ready to charge the three of them. His face showed anger and betrayal; his silver fists were clenched. He grew brighter, causing the air to shimmer and ripple around him.

"Reed . . ." Ben began.

"Wait," Reed said. "He's not in range."

"Just let me . . ." Johnny said.

"Wait!" Reed repeated.

"Sue," Johnny yelled, "get that thing going!"

"That's what I'm doing," she said over her shoulder.

"Then do it faster!" her brother snapped back.

"Okay, shut up!" she yelled. She smacked the side of the metal case, and the dish sprouted up from the transmitter. "It's up!"

The Surfer hovered menacingly, radiating a furious glow. He threw his arms back, unleashing a small tornado of dirt behind him. The back of his board tipped up slightly, then thrust itself forward. He charged like a bull straight toward Reed and the others, a glowing cloud of debris trailing in his wake. Reed looked down at his PDA and triggered the posts again. They all linked online and created the energy field Reed had designed. A quick flash permeated the forest clearing as the posts jammed the signal between the Surfer and his board. The Surfer stopped instantly, and his board began to wobble in the air as his entire body seized and convulsed. The Surfer grew limp and sank through his board, falling hard to the dirty ground below. The once powerful and hovering board fell next to him with a thud.

"Wipeout," Johnny said with a grin.

Sue threw a force field around the lifeless board, making sure it was out of the Surfer's reach. The Four walked over to the fallen Surfer, who lay limp in the dirt and brush. With his power diminished, he no longer radiated energy and his glow disappeared. He appeared tarnished, dirty. The Surfer looked up at Sue with pleading, helpless eyes.

Victor stepped out of the woods and walked toward the fallen silver being. The Surfer turned his head quickly, his eyes narrowing at the sight of Victor Von Doom. The Surfer raised his hand to no effect, the useless digits hanging in the air, his tremendous power gone.

"Not so tough now, are you?" Victor said in a menacing tone before unleashing his powerful electricity on the helpless Surfer. Thick fingers of powerful lightning flew into the Surfer and he writhed in pain, clutching his side as the shock ran through his whole body. Victor's power was scorching the ground around the Surfer, blackening the green leaves and ferns, and still he did not yell out. Nor did Victor stop his barrage of electricity.

"Victor!" Reed yelled, trying to stop the inhumane beating of the fallen Surfer. Reed could see that Victor's eyes were glazed over and shining as the electricity was reflected in them, caught up in the moment of unnecessary violence. Reed stretched out and grabbed Victor's hands, pulling them upward. A few fingers of electricity shot up out of the forest before Victor regained his composure. His steely eyes looked at Reed without a trace of remorse.

Finally, Victor ceased his assault, and actually shrugged, as if the entire affair made no difference to him. "You're the quarterback," he remarked.

Sue carefully approached the unconscious Surfer. His silver skin was now pale, defaced, almost blemished as he lay there, defeated, in the scorched and ruined earth. A shiver ran through her entire body. *He looks so helpless*, she said to herself and the image of a fallen angel flooded her mind. Something broke inside of her and she couldn't stop the tears that swelled in her eyes. They had defeated their foe. The planet was, in theory, safe. But a feeling lingered deep inside of her, an instinct only heightened by the sight of the prone figure on the ground before her. Something told her that their actions today had only made things worse.

14

THE U.S. MILITARY BASE WAS NESTLED DEEP IN THE Arctic, a mystery to even those stationed there. Strong gale winds blew snow and ice around furiously, all but hiding the institution from spy satellites and other international observers. Whiteouts were a common occurrence amid such primal and vicious weather, so far from the shelter of the civilized world. When the winds died down, the base's structure became a bit clearer: one building for housing, one for operations, and a large hangar to house the swiftest and most powerful military jets. The night sky, here at the top of the world, was clear and bright, the silver stars casting a white light across the deep, inky night. Beyond anything within the United States, beyond Guantánamo Bay, this isolated and top secret base in the middle of nowhere was reserved for the U.S. military's most dangerous captives, the ones needing the most persuasion to cooperate. Even the most recalcitrant prisoner could turn helpful here in the center of nothing, with only miles and miles of blistering white to be seen in every direction.

General Hager and Captain Raye watched the arrival of the prisoner from their safe and relatively warm vantage point inside the main entrance of the base. Heavily armed soldiers in thick parkas and gloves unloaded the Surfer. Chains bound his wrists, holding them firmly behind his back. His feet were similarly shackled, with a loose piece of chain between them, allowing him to walk from the transport helicopter to the base. Duct tape was used to keep him blind, unsure of his steps, vulnerable. The Surfer displayed no reaction to the vicious cold as he was moved outside, the soldiers pushing him along with their thick guns, steam escaping from their mouths with each frigid word uttered. Another dozen guards, also heavily armed, stood waiting to receive the prisoner. General Hager grunted with satisfaction at the sight of the captured and bound Surfer.

Reed, Victor, and the others were not privy to the sight, having been brought in under military escort and taken to a conference room in the rear of the facility. Hager surmised that they had served their purpose; he would ship them out of here as soon as the prisoner was secured and he could spare a pilot to fly them away. But for now, they would be kept under guard. Out of his way.

Hager and Raye silently walked the short distance to the rear conference room where the Four were waiting. He was keeping them under close guard, not wanting any surprises until the Surfer was locked safely in the base's special holding cell. But it wasn't long before he heard a commotion and the brisk voices of the guards coming through the partially opened door of the room.

Reed's face showed his obvious concern over the treatment of both his team and the prisoner.

"We had an agreement, General," Reed said, his words heated and loud.

"Calm down," the general replied. "The enemy's been captured. Mission accomplished." He pasted a smile on his face, trying to sound convincing.

"Where is he?" Sue asked, locking eyes with General Hager.

"Contained," the general said.

Victor stepped to the forefront. "And his board?" he asked.

Captain Raye spoke up. "It's in a chamber that continuously scrambles the signal." Victor eyed Raye in a way that made her skin crawl.

Suddenly the air was filled with the sound of heavy wheezing. A chill swept through the room as if someone had just opened a window, letting in the arctic blasts of air. Hager turned to see a short, bald man standing in the doorway. His eyes were shielded behind large mirrored goggles that gripped his pale, thin-skinned skull tightly. A long mink coat was wrapped around his slight shoulders and gathered gently at his feet. One of the man's frail, pale hands emerged from the sea of mink, holding the coat close around his chest. The short pink digits of his hand had long, tapered nails that looked a slightly polished. The wheezing continued as the short man looked around the room, his gaze finally coming to rest on the general.

While the others started at the strange-looking vision in the doorway, General Hager didn't miss a beat. "Mr. Sherman," the general said, trying hard to smile. "Good to see you. We could use your help."

The eerie little man didn't move but stood frozen in the doorway. His voice, when he spoke, held undercurrents of malice. "Take me to it," he wheezed.

General Hager brought his hands together with a loud clap, stirring the room's occupants from their momentary stupor. "If you'll all excuse us," he said, sounding as businesslike as possible, "we have work to do."

Reed approached the general, keeping one eye on the figure in the doorway. "I'd like to be present for questioning," he said.

The general kept walking toward the door, barely acknowledging Reed's request, saying only, "Not going to happen." He led the diminutive man out of the doorway and into the hall, then turned and stopped the five in their tracks with a look. With one gesture from the general the guards in the room followed him out and positioned themselves on the other side of the door. "Please make sure our guests remain here comfortably," Hager said in a clipped tone before shutting the door behind him.

Hager passed through the long, cold hallways of the arctic base, leading Mr. Sherman through a series of armed checkpoints until they reached their destination. Termed the "guest center" on all official documents, the area was little more than a high-tech prison. State-of-the-art locking mechanisms and surveillance equipment made the individual cells impervious to even the idea of escape. A mélange of lights, lasers, tools, and other items of coercion were carefully secreted behind locked cabinet doors. A number of trained intelligence officers, each known officially as a "concierge," were employed at the base to see that each guest earned his keep in providing whatever information was deemed necessary by the military. General Hager carefully dismissed the staff present in the information center, with the exception of his armed escort. Once they were alone, General Hager led Mr. Sherman to the cell holding the Silver Surfer. He punched the secret security code into a small keypad on the wall and the double doors opened swiftly and silently. The two men entered the room.

The cell was a small, square room with padded walls. A small porthole was situated on the wall farthest from the door, displaying the great expanse of white nothingness outside. The Surfer's arms and legs were bound by newly developed restraints that could absorb many types of energy and explosions without effect. The restraints were chained to the floor, thereby rendering movement almost impossible. The Surfer sat on his knees in the empty, cold cell.

He stared ahead silently, impassively, making no sign of acknowledgement that others had entered the room. He seemed focused on some other place, his silver-pooled eyes lost to the details around him. General Hager allowed Mr. Sherman to enter the cell, while he remained in the doorway, watching.

Mr. Sherman doffed his mink coat, which floated to the ground around him. He brought his pale hands together, the tips of his sharp nails resting against one another. His white face lit up at the sight of the silver being, his eyes traveling all over the Surfer's tarnished and dull skin.

"I've always imagined what it would be like to meet a real live alien," Mr. Sherman spoke in a wheeze, just above a whisper. "Ever since I was a child. And now," he said, a thin smile spreading across his face, "here you are." Mr. Sherman slowly circled the bound Surfer as he spoke, observing every inch of the specimen. The Surfer continued to stare into space, oblivious to the words of the small, menacing man near him.

Mr. Sherman stopped directly in front of the Surfer. He was almost at eye level with the bound alien, and spoke directly into his face. "There is *so much* we can learn from each other. Like what powers does that board of yours have, and how do we access them?"

No response, eliciting a sigh from Mr. Sherman. "There are some things that I am not permitted to do because they're considered human-rights violations . . ." he said, letting his voice trail off into the empty space of the cell. They bent over, staring hard at the Surfer's passive face. "Fortunately, you're *not* human."

Back in the rear conference room, the Fantastic Four were stewing about their treatment at the hands of the U.S. military. Guards continued to stand outside the door of the room. Victor kept his distance from the others, staring out the window at the endless white landscape around them. Reed huddled close to Sue, Ben, and Johnny, discussing their current situation.

"Are we prisoners?" Johnny fumed. " 'Cause that just blows."

"Apparently they don't want us interfering with their methods," Reed said, nodding toward the guarded door.

"I hate to think what they're doing to him in there," Sue added, crossing her arms in front of her. The very idea of it gave her a chill.

Ben seemed unconcerned about the Surfer's welfare. "I say he deserves what he gets," he stated loudly.

Sue turned to him with a look of disbelief. "What?! I can't believe you mean that!"

Ben held his rocky hands out in front of him. "I'm just saying. Maybe the general is right about this. The guy was about to destroy the planet. He said so himself."

Sue dismissed Ben's comment immediately. "It doesn't make sense. He protected me from those missiles. Why would he do that?"

Reed agreed with Sue. "There's more going on here. He said he wasn't the destroyer."

Ben waved his hand at Reed. "He could've been lying to mess with our heads."

Reed rubbed his jaw as he spoke. "I just wish we had some way of knowing what's going on in there."

Sue's eyes lit up. "Who says we don't?" she said, giving her brother a knowing look.

A few moments later, Johnny opened the door to the conference room. The two guards, holding large automatic guns, immediately sprung to attention. Their stance was not overly aggressive, but it was clear there was no going past them. Johnny put on his most innocent face.

"Sorry to bother you," he said, holding his hands up. "We were just hoping to get some DVDs to pass the time. Maybe some popcorn?"

"I'll call it in, Mr. Storm," the first guard said.

"Thanks," Johnny replied. "*Semper Fi!*"

"That's the Marine Corps," the second guard remarked, a look of contempt on his face. "We're the Army."

"Sorry," Johnny said, staying in full view of the guards while, out of the corner of his eye, he noted a familiar ripple of air down the hallway. It was his sister, invisible to the human eye, making her covert getaway.

Sue maintained her invisibility as she hurried away from the conference room and down into the main part of the base. She soon entered a long stretch of concrete hallways with numerous locked doors. Focusing intently, she cast a spotlight over each door she encountered, using her powers to make them invisible as well, so that she had visual access to the rooms' contents. She searched several rooms in this fashion until she reached the main intelligence center. Staying close to the walls, she threw her spotlight onto the closed door of the Surfer's cell. She could see the Surfer, bound on the floor, his head against his chest, prostrate in front of Mr. Sherman and General Hager. She felt a catch in her throat when she saw the pitiful condition of the Surfer. His skin was duller, more tarnished than before. She could almost feel his pain. She moved closer to the door.

Just then, Captain Raye entered the intelligence center and punched in a code on the keypad near the door. It opened quickly, just as Mr. Sherman's wheezy voice echoed throughout the room. "Let's not do that again," he said. Sue once again felt a chill at the malevolent tone of the strange man's voice.

Captain Raye entered the cell. Sue snuck in quickly behind her, moving as quietly as she could. "Victor Von Doom needs to speak with you, General," the captain said, her tone officious and matter of fact. General Hager nodded in her direction and then motioned Mr. Sherman to the door. They all left the room, leaving Sue alone with the damaged Surfer. She heard the doors lock, then the weakened, ethereal voice of the Surfer. "I know you are there."

Sue materialized and rushed to his side. She bent down, instinctively wanting to comfort him. She touched his head softly. "The people of our world don't condone this kind of treatment," she said, images of Abu Ghraib suddenly flashing in her mind. The words sounded hollow, even to her. "Are you hurt?" she asked.

"No," the Surfer replied. She could tell he was not being truthful but he raised his head from his chest and made eye contact with her. She thought she saw a look of recognition before his face returned to its calm, expressionless visage.

"What is your name?" Sue asked. "You must have a name. I'm Susan." He looked confused, unsure of the meaning of her words. Being so close to him, even with him in such a beaten state, stirred within her powerful memories of their encounter in the Black Forest. Once again she fought the urge to protect him, to shelter him from the dire circumstances around them. His calm, gentle demeanor only enhanced those protective feelings. The Surfer had said he was not the destroyer, and she wanted desperately to believe him. Looking deep into his eyes, she doubted that such a creature could willingly perform such violent acts. She cleared her throat to speak. "You said you weren't the one to destroy our world. Then who is?" she asked.

The Surfer's expression changed then, as if a shadow had entered the room. "The one I serve," he said quietly.

Susan felt her heart beating faster. "Who do you serve?" she asked urgently. She watched as his expression grew pained, a curtain falling over his entire face. He fell silent and his gaze drifted away from her, into the thin air. "I want to help you," she pleaded, "but in order to do that, you have to tell me the truth. Please." Sue searched his eyes for some acknowledgment of her request. She wanted to trust him. Everything in her was telling her to do so. But unless he confided in her, unless he explained himself, she knew there was nothing she could do. For him, or the group, or the planet.

The Surfer dropped his head back to his chest. Sue felt defeated; her words had had no effect. She wasn't getting through to him, or he wasn't allowing her to. But suddenly a spark grew from his chest. Sue took a step back, watching the light grow into a swirling mist of energy and light. She felt her face grow warm as she was once again bathed in the tremendous power of the Surfer. The small cone of swirling light stayed near his chest and then grew out from it, filling the space between the Surfer and the mesmerized Sue. The light danced as it formed a picture, a hologram to show the memory the Surfer was trying to convey.

The hologram showed a vortex of staggering size, made up of both energy and organic matter. Points of light flashed and reflected from it as the vortex churned its way through space, its obvious power seen in the pulsing, throbbing, angry clouds all around it. The hunger of the vortex was limitless; everything it touched was consumed. Asteroids shattered, stars disappeared, and entire plants were subsumed in an instant. The destroyer was unstoppable, ravenous, its fearsome power darker than the endless space that surrounded it.

The Surfer began to speak again, narrating the horrifying image in front of her. "It is known by many names. My people called it *Gah Lak Tus*, the Devourer of Worlds."

The hologram projected the image of a planet just like Earth, with lush greens and blues, rotating proudly in a pocket of deep space. Its isolation came to a swift and brutal end as Gah Lak Tus moved into the space around it, the darkness collapsing in on itself as the destroyer consumed the energy of the stars in the planet's orbit. Even though no sound can exist in space, Gah Lak Tus seemed to roar as it sped closer to the planet, its hunger growing, engulfing everything in its path. Suddenly the surface of the planet became evident, the atmosphere dispersing and parting like the Red Sea. Silver craters littered the landscape and could be seen scarring the planet's surface, even from space. The craters started to glow and hum, shaking violently, putting off their destructive power in short flashes of light. Just then, huge elongated streams of volcanic molten rock gushed up from the craters to the swirling vortex, their fiery plumes of heated energy giving the vortex power and nourishment. The planet began to melt as it was consumed by the vortex, turning into nothing but stray matter and ash as it gave up its precious core to the swirling, voluminous, ravenous Gah Lak Tus.

Sue stared at the hologram, horrified. The vortex had consumed the planet they way a person might punch a straw into an orange to suck out the juice. No thought, no remorse, no mercy. Only hunger. "The craters," she said. "They let it draw the thermal energy from the planet's core."

The Surfer acknowledged her words with a slight nod of his head. "It must feed on energy to survive. Both thermal and organic."

Horror registered on Sue's face. Her heart was racing. "Organic? You're talking about plants? Animals? People?" She could barely get the last word out. The Surfer was showing her acts that were nothing short of interplanetary genocide. It was too overwhelming to process. All the compassion she felt for the beaten silver being dissipated in the face of such total annihilation. She turned her rage on him. "That's monstrous. How could you willingly serve such a thing?" she yelled.

The Surfer flinched at the anger behind her words. His voice grew softer as he turned away. "Because I must." He let his head fall back to his chest as the hologram disappeared in a swift swirl of light. The room once again fell silent and cold.

Sue struggled to maintain her composure. "Doesn't it bother you at all? The worlds, the people you've helped destroy?"

The Surfer stayed silent while Sue waited for some kind of response, one that could possibly make any sense. His face remained expressionless but Sue thought she could feel some kind of struggle going on within him. But Sue needed more. More of an explanation. "Why did you try to protect me?" she asked.

The even, calm tone of her voice surprised the Surfer. Her anger was already dissolving—or she was concealing it. "You are much like someone I once knew. Someone dear to me," he finally said.

The humanity of his remark made an impression on her. For all the horrors Sue had seen today, for all the violence the Surfer had displayed, his words were not deceptive. The Surfer did not seem to lie. "Then you can feel compassion," she said. The Silver Surfer only looked up at her, his calm face a sharp contrast to the charged emotions running through Sue's body. She wanted to shake him from his placid appearance, wanted him to understand, or at least admit to, the horrors he had witnessed. But he stayed silent, helpless.

Sue walked away from the Surfer and over to the porthole window. She couldn't look at him. Not right now. The hopelessness of the situation weighed upon her as she struggled to find a way out of this. She had to get back to Reed and tell him what she had learned. But part of her wanted to keep this from him, to shield him from how they were all going to die. Outside, the endless white horizon stretched out before her.

"Could you stop the Destroyer from coming if you wanted to?" she asked over her shoulder, keeping her gaze on the miles of arctic land around them.

The Surfer answered her quickly, like a child who longed to be rewarded. "It is not I who draws the Destroyer here. It is the beacon."

"What beacon?" she asked.

"The source of my power," he said.

The board? she thought to herself. *The earth is doomed to a fiery, apocalyptic demise because of a surfboard?*

"Take joy in the last few hours you have left," the Surfer added. "For it is nearly here."

His final words filled the room. Sue's reaction was calm, almost as if she was in a slight state of shock. Her expression was not unlike the one she had witnessed so often on the Silver Surfer's face, a visage, perhaps, of defense in the face of such overwhelming destruction and violence. Her gaze searched the frozen tundra for explanations or reasons, but she found nothing. Only a useless wasteland, a repetition of cold, white ice, a stark contrast to the future that was about to arrive.

Outside the porthole, the miles and miles of arctic land seemed to stretch out forever, alone and shivering at the top of the world. Eventually the land and sheets of ice reached a horizon, a thin tissue of darkness sprinkled with silver stars, the beginning of outer space. The slim film of atmosphere made the heavens seem within reach, touchable, even at their great distance. At that moment the Earth did not seem so distant from its silent brothers, the planets circling within view: the cold, unblinking moon; the red star Mercury; the glowing rings of Saturn. Just behind that ethereal planet a series of flashes set off the expanse of deep space. The rings of Saturn began to bend and warp, before they were eventually pulled from the planet by a strong vortex. The Destroyer took them greedily, only wanting more.

In a matter of minutes, the planet known as Saturn was gone, a relic of history.

Gah Lak Tus continued on its path, heading toward Earth and its inevitable destruction.

15

SUE COULD BARELY FORCE THE WORDS OUT OF HER mouth. Back in the conference room, she told Reed and the others what the Surfer had shared with her through his holographic memory. She told them everything: about Gah Lak Tus, the endless number of planets destroyed, the millions of people killed. She watched the reactions on her teammates' faces— expressions that swung from fear and horror back to resolution and determination. Suddenly she felt comforted by their presence, by the collective strength of the group. She remembered that she was in the company of heroes.

"It'll be here in a few hours," she said in conclusion. "He said the board is drawing it here."

"We have to get the board and lead it away from here," Reed surmised. "Before it's too late."

Johnny thought that could be a lot harder to do than to say. "You think the general will go for that?" he asked.

"He won't have a choice," Reed replied.

* * *

At that moment, the general was walking down a hallway with Victor Von Doom. He'd allowed his armed guard to escort Victor from the conference room so they could talk in private, per Victor's request. The general did not want Richards to know he had struck a deal with Victor behind his back. *I am the quarterback of this team*, the general reminded himself. *I have the authority to do what I want.*

As they walked toward another containment facility, the droning voice of Victor Von Doom was already trying the patience of General Hager. The armed escort walked behind them, alert and ready for any disturbances. They passed several armed checkpoints within the facility on their way to another top secret lab.

"I helped deliver the alien to you, as promised," Victor continued. "Now keep your end of the bargain."

The general held up his hands. "You can do your tests on the board," he said. "But under armed guard. In my presence only."

Victor scowled as they turned a corner and arrived at the containment lab. The general once again dismissed the armed guards and he and Victor entered the sleek, modern room filled with state-of-the-art equipment, enough of it to rival even Richards's back at the Baxter Building. Victor's gaze moved over a number of new toys he no doubt wanted to get his hands on, but his eyes stopped on one object in particular: the Surfer's board. There, motionless on a pedestal beneath thick glass, sat the thin, shining piece of weaponry. It still radiated a strong, reflective silver hue. Only the Surfer had suffered from their separation.

Victor eyed the surfboard ravenously. He could feel it was the most powerful weapon in the universe. Its metallic hue was not entirely unlike his own. Standing so close to it, Victor could feel a vibrant hum course through his body. A slight sense of euphoria permeated his thoughts and feelings. It felt like the board was calling out to him, like it belonged to him.

"Thank you, General," Victor said, his eyes never leaving the silver board. "But I'm afraid the truth is—as much as I hate to admit it—something Reed said is right." Suddenly Victor turned on the general, unleashing his powerful electric currents all over the unsuspecting man. Hager collapsed against a wall, his clothes letting off trails of smoke. Victor easily shot down the armed guard as well, his chest scorched and still burning by the time his lifeless body hit the floor. "This is a tachyon pulse emitter," he said to no one, placing a small electronic device on the forearm of his metallic skin. Victor's body armor began to hum and glow, giving off the powerful and seductive tachyon energy. The Surfer's board also began to glow and then, suddenly, sprung to life, rising off the pedestal and into the air.

Victor raised his hand toward the board. The thick

glass surrounding it rippled like water and separated, allowing the board to come to him. Victor stepped gingerly on the board and instantly felt it: the surging and powerful energy, the full-throated euphoria of being connected to every living thing. Victor could feel everything on a molecular level, could see the strains and bonds that kept matter intact, could see how to bend them at his will. Victor had long harbored the secret ambition to be a god and now, standing on the board, he felt that dream had come true. That this was meant to be.

On the floor next the wall, General Hager stirred. His hair stood on end and his fingers tingled—the aftereffects of Victor's strong electromagnetic blast. The general looked up to see Victor glowing, lost to the power of the board. He pulled out his gun, armed with metal-tipped bullets, and aimed squarely at Victor's shining chest. Victor noticed the general the way he would a fly. With a slight wave of his hand the armor-shredding bullets turned to a fine dust that drifted lightly to the floor. He narrowed his eyes at the prone figure of the general, who was trying to crawl away, out the door. With a movement of Victor's fingers the general halted. His body became rigid, caught in Victor's invisible grip. Like a puppet the general was lifted off the ground and spun around, suspended in midair while Victor locked his eyes on the petrified man. Victor looked deep inside the body of the general, sensing the molecular construction of his internal organs. He began making alterations, experimenting with his new power.

A thick trail of blood dripped out of General Hager's ear as he writhed in agony, as pain lanced his entire body. Victor played with the general's epidermis and his once clear, dark skin shriveled like wet paper and fell the ground below him in a puddle of blood and cells. His throat constricted as Victor brought his lungs and heart up from his chest, the general making wet choking noises, unable to move or defend himself. Blood vessels on his face and arms popped like grapes in a vise. His fingers turned deep purple as they pooled with blood. Violent tremors kicked his legs and feet. The base of his brain swelled and finally exploded, partially covering the wall behind him just as his aorta collapsed and the general sent out one long, final cough thick with phlegm and blood. Victor let the bloody general fall to the floor, the insides of his body pooling around his lifeless form. Victor stood motionless on the board, impressed that the gory act had required little more than a thought to complete. He turned to the wall of the lab and with a single clap of his hands sent the entire side of the military base flying into the white, barren landscape. Explosions rocketed the structure as the fire reached out to the ice.

Victor sped through the destruction, laughing, watching the flames begin to engulf the lab and the entire side of the isolated military base. The flames looked radiant against the background of sheer white. He rose on his board, higher and higher, oblivious to the cold, crackling with energy and power. He shot off toward a deep black Arctic sky filled with stars, another silver speck in an already crowded and now deadly nightscape.

16

A LARGE EXPLOSION ROCKED THE MILITARY BASE, SHAK-
ing the whole structure to its frozen foundations. The
bitterly cold weather had made the steel walls rigid
and brittle, and they cracked like plastic in the face
of Victor's fearsome new power. The explosions in the
containment lab reverberated throughout the entire
compound and the Fantastic Four felt the blasts all
the way in the rear conference room. They watched
the thick glass of the window there splinter and crack
while dust fell from the ceiling like snow.

In the pandemonium that ensued, Reed, Sue,
Johnny, and Ben rushed out of the room, following their armed guards down several hallways to the
containment facility that once held the board. Upon
seeing the destruction, none of them had any doubt
that Victor had caused this. His disappearance from
the conference room minutes before the blasts had not
gone unnoticed by any of them.

Ben led the way, pushing scorched and burning debris out of their path. Johnny ignited his power and
drew most of the remaining flames into his own burn-

ing core, dousing the hungry fire. Sue used small discs to envelop the equipment that was still burning, containing it in her force field, depriving the flames of oxygen and thereby smothering them.

Reed had sidestepped most of the damage and now made his way past the empty glass containment case, only to see Victor speeding away from the site. Reed lost sight of him as Victor's speed turned him into just another silver speck in an already crowded sky. Reed rushed back in to see his team extinguishing the last of the flames. The lab was ruined. He surmised that the blackened equipment could barely be used even for scrap metal now. It was then that Reed's eyes fell on the slightly charred remains of the body of General Hager. Even with the fire damage, the gore was apparent, as was, soon, the smell. He fought the urge to retch and joined his team, who were already standing by the empty glass case.

"We've got to get it back," Reed said, his tone urgent.

"We need the Surfer," Sue stated. "He's the only one who knows its powers."

Ben shook his head. "Are you nuts?" he asked, keeping one eye on the frozen tundra now visible through the missing wall of the lab. "Even if we break him out of here, how are we going to catch up with Victor?"

Reed's face lit up. "Leave that to me." He pulled out his PDA and the Fantastic Four logo came up on the small screen. He punched it immediately, sending a signal back to his lab at the Baxter Building. There, in the darkened space, a large object hidden beneath a thick plastic tarp sprang to life. The object had been waiting silently for weeks, as Reed had busied himself with other things: the wedding, the geographic anomalies, the sensor he'd built for Hager. But the time for waiting was over. The strong, almost silent engine could be heard igniting, an electronic purr echoing in the lab.

Ben once again took the lead as the Four moved through the maze of hallways and prisons in the center of the Arctic base. The soldiers were in disarray following Victor's attack and the death of General Hager and were much too concerned with that to pay much attention to the actions of the group. The Four were simply no longer a military concern now that the entire base was under attack.

Sue led the team to the Surfer's cell. Ben eyed the keypad on the side of the door, shrugged quickly, and let loose. His large, rocky fist made quick work of the door; it caved in under his powerful punch. An alarm started to sound immediately, adding to the general chaos in the base.

Ben ran into the cell, and found the Surfer still chained in his special restraints. "Pal, this is the luckiest day of your life," he said.

The Surfer looked up at Ben, his face still expressionless. It was not until he saw Sue arrive in the room that a glimmer of recognition crossed his dull, tarnished face.

"It's all right," she said to him. "Come on." Ben worked quickly on the restraints, careful not to hurt the Surfer's limbs. He lifted the Surfer from the ground and helped him out of the cell and into the hallway. They all took off running, eager to be as far away from the cell as possible when the guards came in response to the alarm.

They rounded a corner and came face-to-face with the general's aide, Captain Raye.

Her usual calm demeanor was obviously shaken by the chaos of the day, and the sight of the Four helping the Surfer escape did nothing to help that. She reached for her weapon and drew it quickly, taking a protective stance. "What the hell is going on?" she yelled loudly, over the still ringing alarms. "Where is General Hager?"

Reed stepped forward with his hands up, not wanting to further startle the captain. "He's dead," Reed said softly. A look of disbelief crossed her beautiful face as she raised her gun higher.

"And if we don't get him out of here," Ben added, pointing at the Surfer, "we're all going to be, too."

"I can't let you do that," she said, her voice shaking a bit, along with the hand holding the gun.

* * *

Johnny watched Frankie Raye's and felt a twinge of compassion for the stricken woman. She had obviously been very close to General Hager, and it couldn't have been easy hearing about his death. He had to do something. "Frankie," he said softly, "the world is literally at stake here." He reached out for her hand, the one holding the gun. "Trust me," he said. "Please." Johnny managed to wrap his hand around hers slowly and bring the gun down to her side. He looked deep into her startlingly blue eyes and could see the hurt and confusion there. He would help her, he vowed to himself—once this was all over with.

The captain regained her composure just as a team of armed soldiers began making their way down the hall. Sue concentrated for a moment and turned her team and the Surfer invisible, giving the appearance that Captain Raye was standing alone in the hallway. The soldiers arrived at the captain's side, looking to her for direction, as she outranked them and the orders were hers to give.

Captain Raye hesitated for just a moment before telling them to head toward level two, a section on the other side of the base. She followed the soldiers on the wild goose chase, giving the Four the room they needed. Captain Raye looked back for a moment to watch the group reappear before she, too, exited the hallway.

"We need to get to the roof," Reed said once they had fully materialized. "It should be here by now."

A look of confusion crossed Ben's face. "What should be here by now?" he asked.

"My hobby," Reed said with a smirk.

They made their way up the stairwell to a door marked ROOF ACCESS. Ben put his fist through the door, sending it flying out of the doorjamb and onto the snow-covered roof. They all braced themselves for the cold and joined the ruined door outside.

The Four stopped in their tracks when they saw it.

There, hovering in the air, was Reed's latest hobby.

More of a sleek jet than a car or boat, the vehicle, with its smooth, curved lines, was obviously designed for speed. The hull, made of burnished adamantium, glowed in the moonlight. The shape was similar to that of a manta ray, its dipped sides curving down into flat, short wings on either side of the craft. The open-air seating in the jet looked similar to that in a canoe, its elongated form allowing for a cockpit in the front with one seat for the pilot, two seats behind the cockpit, and one in the rear. Each section looked self-sufficient and separate from the rest of the craft. The flat design of the jet was years ahead of its time. The front hull displayed the familiar number-four logo, the banner of the Fantastic Four.

"Holy crap!" Ben exclaimed.

"Reed . . ." Johnny stammered, his face lighting up like a kid at Christmas. "This . . . is the coolest thing you've ever done."

His future brother-in-law only smiled in response. Johnny couldn't wait to get his hands on this, his eyes crawling all over the exterior before spying a rather familiar yet subtly placed Dodge logo.

He shot Reed a look. "Hemi?"

Reed shrugged, struggling to make himself heard over the vehicle's powerful, purring engine. "Of course . . . Ben, get in! Johnny, you fly behind us!"

Fly behind us?

Reed and Sue began helping the Surfer—who still wore a look of perfect astonishment at the actions of Johnny and his teammates—up and into the sleek machine, with Ben following. Meaning no more room. *Uh uh, no way.*

"Dude, you have *got* to let me drive!" Johnny shouted at Reed in protest.

"Forget it!" Ben shot back. "*I'm* the best pilot here, I should drive!"

"Guys . . ." Sue began to plead, attempting to defuse the situation.

"Are you kidding me?!" Johnny flared. "We'll be lucky if this thing can stay in the air carrying your two-ton butt."

"Guys, come on . . ." Sue said.

"I could fly circles around you blindfolded!" yelled Ben.

"Shut up and move it!"

Reed's unexpected outburst instantly silenced their

escalating argument. Rare as it was, Johnny had learned early on that whenever Reed lost it, boy, did he mean business. Plus, better to stay on Reed's good side if he ever wanted to have a crack at driving this thing before Ben could, even if now wasn't the best time.

"Right," was all Johnny said.

"Yes, sir," Ben piped up, defeated, quickly climbing into the cab.

"Flame on!" Johnny shouted, and his body was instantly engulfed in a familiar inferno. Reed was already in the driver's seat, taking hold of the navigation controls and guiding the vehicle off the roof, taking to the cold air and jetting off into the ink-black night.

As Johnny followed, out of the corner of his eye he saw the rooftop burst open and soldiers spilling and racing out of the opening. *Sucks to be you, guys,* he thought with a smile. *You're a day late and a dollar short.*

17

THE SLEEK NEW JET CARRIED THE FOUR QUICKLY AWAY from the barren wastelands of the Arctic, crossing the sky and soon entering the airspace over Asia. Reed was quietly impressed with his own craftsmanship; the controls of the jet were working smoothly, and its speed could top two hundred miles per hour. Other systems aboard, however, still felt a little clunky to him. He made mental notes to check on the radiation sensors and navigation systems. They showed no sign of any anomalies, and Victor should be putting out massive amounts of energy. The kind of power Victor now had should be showing up *somewhere*. *Unless he's figured out how to hide*, Reed thought. He was hoping that Victor had not yet mastered the power of the board. He thought that lack of precision would be their one shot at defeating Victor, if he was still unaware of the raw power in his possession. But now, as Reed's eyes surveyed the many quiet instruments across his cockpit console, he feared they no longer had that advantage.

The rest of the group was slightly distracted by the surprise existence of the jet. Sue recalled how mar times she'd begged Reed to find them some private way to travel, and now he had done it. Without a word to her, he had done it. Sue sat about a foot behind Reed's right shoulder, next to the Surfer. Ben had shoved himself into the back section, behind them all. As the flew, their elation about Reed's new vehicle faded, and a silence fell over the group as they realized that a hard struggle lay ahead of them.

Ben Grimm broke the silence with his deep, gravelly voice. "Okay. We're now officially enemies of America. Victor is out there somewhere with unlimited power. And we've got a giant, intergalactic force that's about to destroy our planet in less than twenty-four hours. Did I miss anything?" His words were meant to be sarcastic, but he sounded defeated.

"I forgot to TiVo *24*," Johnny quipped from outside, in a effort to dispel the gloomy atmosphere inside the jet.

Ben ignored his comment. "So what do we do now?" he asked. Ben's question seemed to mirror the thoughts of Sue and her teammates as they each struggled to think of a way to stop both Victor and the imminent threat of the destroyer. Everything they had been through over the past few days—the geographic anomalies, the ruined wedding, the encounters with the Surfer, Johnny's new ability to switch powers with the others, learning that Victor was alive and once again a threat, not to mention the gruesome death of General Hager—all these events were leading them to this place. To a final confrontation. How and when that would occur was still a mystery to everyone, so Ben's query was left hanging in the air, unanswered.

"Norrin Radd." It was the ethereal voice of the Surfer, coming from the middle of the craft.

Reed and Sue turned, a bit startled, as the Surfer had been silent since they'd broken him out of Hager's containment cell.

"I was once called Norrin Radd," the Surfer repeated.

"That's one weird-ass name," Johnny remarked, looking from the outside at Ben.

Ben stared at Johnny for a split second in disbelief. "Shut up," he responded, shaking his rocky head in frustration.

Sue recovered her voice and gave him a smile. "It's nice to meet you, Norrin."

The Surfer continued staring at Sue, his deep-pooled eyes now looking for some kind of recognition in her soft, human face. "Serving the destroyer meant sparing my world and saving the one I loved," he offered as explanation for his actions. Once he had made his confession, the Surfer looked down at his tarnished hands and became quiet once again.

Sue understood his intentions. She had sensed that the Surfer was not a malevolent force since their encounter in the Black Forest. She wanted to believe he was a victim of circumstance, someone whose duty to the ones he loved made him merely an object of sacrifice. She could understand that, the need to protect the ones you loved. She had seen it cross all their faces in the heat of battle. It was the foundation for the camaraderie of the group that was also like a family. Sue held no doubt in her mind that should the situation arise, she would undoubtedly make the same choices the Surfer had made.

"Norrin," she said, "please help us save our world, as you have your own." She knew her words had touched him, as she could see his face change. His brow furrowed and his eyes, usually bright, dimmed a bit. He seemed to struggle with her plea, perhaps fearful of what such a decision could cost him—or his homeland.

The alien once known as Norrin Radd looked out the window of the jet, unsure of what to say. Of all the worlds he had seen, all the ones he'd helped destroy, this place was the most like his home. It had not been easy for him to come here, to see the lush greens of the land and the radiant blues of the ocean, and not think of everything he had left behind. The familiar sights of this place had rendered within him strong feelings of isolation and longing for his own world, for a place he could never see again. Even now, without the board to establish within him some connection to living things, he felt those emotions. But just because his fate was sealed didn't mean that this beautiful world had to suffer. He couldn't let that happen, not to this place, and not to her.

The Surfer turned back to Sue. Her eyes were still focused on him, pleading. He gave her a silent acquiescence, a gesture only she seemed to understand.

Ben broke up their wordless exchange, apparently frustrated by the group's lack of resolve.

"We could barely beat Victor before," he said from behind them. "With this guy's powers, he's unstoppable."

"So let's just use Reed's tachyon jamming thinga-ma-jig," Johnny said. "It worked on Norbert here."

"Norrin," Sue corrected.

"Whatever," replied Johnny.

"Victor would have compensated for that," said Reed.

The Surfer turned back to the large man who seemed to be made of rocks. He could sense that his physical strength was formidable, but his mind less so. "The power of the board is overwhelming, almost euphoric," the Surfer explained. "It is not something one willingly gives up. Especially if power is all one craves. Does this describe him?"

The ones who called themselves the Fantastic Four merely exchanged glances with one another, confirming the worst. "We are so screwed," Johnny said. A curious, yet obtuse response.

Suddenly the relative calm of the cockpit was shattered by a tremendous shock wave.

Light flooded into the jet, a cosmic cascade of energy that almost blinded them. Reed held on to the steering mechanism tightly, trying to maintain control as waves of energy rolled over them, tossing them like a ship in a stormy sea. The jet shook violently as its passengers were thrown about in their seats. Ben slammed his head against the back wall of the jet, creating a large dent in the metal. Sue threw a force field around the craft, but it wasn't strong enough. The jet continued to shake and the navigation equipment popped, on the verge of shorting out altogether. Reed struggled to keep the jet upright, diverting more power to the thrusters and engine. He stared out the cockpit window and found the source of the great disturbance. In front of them stood Victor Von Doom, shining and resplendent on the Surfer's board. His skin glowed with power as his hands extended toward the new craft, fighting Reed for control.

He saw Sue fighting to maintain her force field in an effort to offer the team some protection from Victor's powerful wrath. A thick stream of blood began to slowly drip from her nose.

Suddenly the jet took a strong dive as Reed started evasive maneuvers to avoid Victor's grasp. He could see Johnny, fully aflame, riding right by their side, sending a stream of fire toward Von Doom's board to try to break his fearsome grip on the jet.

The Fantastic Four sped quickly through the night sky, with Victor right on their tail. They soared through the Gullin Monoliths, the tall, austere mountains appearing black against the shadows of night. Von Doom, remarkably fast on the silver board, gestured toward one of the peaks. The ancient mountain cracked and fell toward Reed's jet. He pulled aside just in time to avoid a collision and the rocky edifice fell to the ground just below them.

Reed could hear the crash of the mountain below, a deep shudder rising from the crust of the landscape, a shower of pebbles and dust scratching the underside of the jet. The steering controls were turning a bit sluggish and the engine was showing signs of strain from Reed's evasive piloting. The navigation systems were almost totally shot, buckling under the strength of Victor's attack. Reed feared the new engines would also give out, having been used at full throttle for so long. The jet, while compact, was simply too cumbersome for such tricky maneuvering and fast flying. He had built it more as a transport than a combat weapon. He knew he would have to resort to Plan B.

"Hold on!" Reed yelled as he threw a number of switches. Components emerged in each section of the craft and extended into position. A smaller version of Reed's steering mechanism extended into Sue's lap.

She locked eyes with Reed, who nodded as he pushed the last button, splitting the sleek jet into three separate vehicles: the front section holding Reed, the middle section holding Sue and the Surfer, and the tail section holding Ben. The smaller jets, each resembling a small submersible, had stronger maneuvering capabilities. Reed surmised that only by separating could they have a chance at outmaneuvering Victor and the surfboard.

Reed watched the other components of the jet cast off. His design and construction worked perfectly. Ben and Sue easily maneuvered away from each other, drawing Victor's fire into three separate directions. Reed watched Johnny hurl a barrage of fireballs at Victor while Sue and the Surfer took to the higher ground, behind a thicket of clouds. Reed felt some concern about leaving Sue alone with Norrin Radd; Victor would need to destroy the Surfer if he was to keep the board permanently, and Reed didn't want Sue's jet to be any more of a target than it already was.

He careened through the sky in the front compartment of the jet and dove down once again, toward the now visible Great Wall of China. Ben followed suit in his own craft, giving Reed's jet plenty of room but keeping protective watch on his blind side. *Ben always has my back*, Reed thought. *Friends 'til the end*, Ben always said. Even if that end was coming tonight.

Reed flew so low to the ground that he could make out the indentations of the stones that made up the Great Wall. The moon cast long shadows over the structure, making the wall appear half-hidden from the fight above.

Victor watched the three jets with amusement, impressed once again with Reed's ingenuity. But his goodwill didn't last long. With a single wave of his hand, Victor unleashed the stones from the Great Wall, pulling them easily from the ancient mortar. The stone missiles flew obediently toward their mark, raining dirt and boulders over Reed and Ben's flight path. Reed dove lower to dodge the stones and Ben pulled up, taking to the higher air to avoid the deadly debris.

As Victor watched his prey try to elude the flying stones, he felt a current of air coming up swiftly from behind him. He turned to see Sue piloting her small part of the jet, aimed right for his head. Victor dropped immediately and she flew right over him, nearly decapitating him in midair with the wing of her small craft.

Victor recovered quickly, using the power of the board to speed up and begin chasing the section holding Sue and the Surfer. He flew on the currents of the swift engine's exhaust, ignoring the turbulence and fumes, gaining on her quickly. The board's speed was incredible and navigated the cold night air with ease, as if nothing could stop it. *She always liked to be chased,*

Victor thought. *And now I'll have her. Finally.* Victor was just about to reach Sue's jet when a bright, thick stream of living flame flew up between them, burning Victor's hand. Victor could see Johnny providing cover as his sister attempted to escape, another futile protective gesture to keep Victor at bay.

Just then, Ben's section of the jet launched up from below, slamming into the underside of the board, sending Victor spinning through the sky. Ben could see Victor on top of the board, twirling like a toy top, a silver speck trapped in a blender of air. The violent rotation, however, was stopped by one single thought from Victor's mind.

Victor ascended then into the dawning day, letting the board take him higher into the air. He continued rising, watching the landscape below and the jets and the Human Torch fall away quickly, becoming insects hovering in dirty air. He rose higher and higher, drawn to great heights by the euphoric power of the board. He could feel the sun, though it lay waking halfway around the world. He could sense the tides in the water, though they swam oceans away. He could smell the air, each living molecule of it, and he could feel it whipping all around him in a meager display of supplication and worship. Suspended and cradled by the board, Victor could feel everything in the world move and shudder, warp and bend to his whim. Every living thing on the planet was humbled in his wake, prostate before him. He could feel it all and wanted nothing more than to gather it entirely, down to every last cell. Herd the entire living organic spectrum and corral it into his grasp. And then squeeze.

He turned back to the meddling bits of Reed's craft, trying to circle around him in a futile attempt to contain him. But the power of the board was not to be contained. It was to be unleashed. Victor raised his hands, glowing madly from the ambition he now felt. "My turn," he said but his voice, deep and universal, was no longer recognizable, no longer of this world.

He brought his hands together in an almighty clap. The energy blooming from his hands pulled together in a godly display of light and electricity. The entire horizon was alight with his power and fury as if dawn was breaking in half. Victor rained vengeance down upon those who dared try to thwart him. The sonic boom from his powerful blast rattled the Great Wall and the Gullin Monoliths. It hid the moon, punished the waking sun. It was as if the entire Earth shuddered under the gaze of Victor's endless power.

Victor felt every inch of his scarred face smile as he watched the three jets and Johnny's extinguished human form tremble before the awesome display of energy before they were thrown, unconscious, out across the landscape, falling to the earth like forgotten stars.

18

THE WORLD CHANGED IN AN INSTANT, AS IT OFTEN does.

One moment Sue was piloting her section of Reed's experimental craft, and the next she simply wasn't. She remembered a display of lights and a barrage of colors and sounds, some of which felt like they were new, just invented, shades and hues she had never before seen.

Her first instinct was a calm, natural one—My, *how beautiful*—before the violence set in.

A strong gust of wind cracked the windshield in front of her and took all the sound away from her ears. She could hear only a dull, subtle ringing then, and when she looked over at the Surfer she saw that his usually calm visage was changed. His hands were suspended in front of him, his deeply pooled silver eyes wide at what they were witnessing. She could remember thinking something inappropriate—*Finally, a different expression*—before she realized what she was seeing: fear.

The once powerful being known as the Silver Surfer was showing fear.

That was when her heart climbed into her throat

and she couldn't breathe. That was when she knew they were falling. The blinking lights and warning alarms of the control panel were distant ringing bells; she couldn't hear them. She could only see the ground coming upon them, fast. She tried to concentrate, tried to form a field around them to offer some protection from the impact. Then, nothing at all.

The small piece of jet was still smoking, a thin wisp of black cloud rising up into the dull, sun-washed air. Morning had come, the sun high and far away, as if it was keeping its distance from the violence on Earth. The Surfer pulled Sue's body along the dirty street, nursing a limp that almost caused him to fall to the ground. He stared at the large building behind them and recognized it as a place of worship. Citizens were standing in the doorways, witnesses to the sudden crash. They, too, kept their distance, unsure of what they were seeing.

The Surfer lay Sue's unconscious body near a deserted Shanghai market street. The stalls were closed up and the few people who were out in the early morning scurried quickly to their destinations, avoiding the sight of the strange silver alien and the sleeping white woman. The Surfer eased his injured leg to the side as he too, took a seat on the ground, weary from the battle. He had never seen power like the one he had just witnessed. He had no idea the board was capable of that. He had seen carnage before, but usually from the presence of Gah Lak Tus, the Destroyer. And while the board was connected to that power, never had he seen it so violently displayed.

He cradled Sue's head in his lap, brushing her blond hair away from her face. Blood oozed from a cut on her forehead and ran in a delicate path to her eyebrow and then down the side of her face. He touched her cheek lightly, remembering Shalla Bal, the one he left so long ago. But memory, he knew, had a way of making time seem weak, powerless. What he left so long ago could be sitting with him here and now. Memory took only a matter of seconds to make it so.

Sue's eyes fluttered and then opened. She awoke to find herself cradled by the Silver Surfer, her head protected from the cold, hard street. She could smell the burning smoke mixed with the humid wetness of dawn. Strangely, she felt quite calm. She looked up to see Norrin Radd staring intently at her, a look of relief briefly crossing his face. The intimacy of the moment touched her deeply. Their connection was not romantic, like what she felt with Reed, nor was it the bond she felt with her brother, Johnny. But she did feel drawn to him, perhaps as one warrior to another, and the need to protect him was somehow never far from her mind when she was in his presence. Only now he was protecting her. She reached up and touched his hand, to convey her gratitude. He helped her stand, slowly, she unsure of her footing and he still nursing his injured leg. Sue noticed that he winced in pain, his silver eyes narrow, when he tried to place his weight on it. It was only the second time she'd seen his face show expression.

Sue led him to the corner of a building, helping him lean on it for support. She looked back to see her section of the jet smoking but still intact. Once she dealt with Norrin's injury, she might be able to get it working again. She noticed a cardboard box in the doorway of a stall across the street and went over to it, looking for something to make a splint for his leg. She took a few deep breaths, hoping the intake of air might help clear her head. The base of her skull throbbed and nausea burned in her stomach. Crossing the street, she tried to remember what she could: the elongated craft separating into individual components, the dogfight in the air, Victor's rabid attack and his seemingly limitless power. She wondered where Reed, Ben, and her brother were; she hoped that they'd also survived the fight.

Sue kneeled before the half-opened box. Chinese lettering was stamped on the rough cardboard in faded red ink. She opened the two flaps and found brightly colored silk fabrics, scarves, and perhaps a heavy garment or two. She wasn't sure they would be of much use, but it was all they had. She'd have to make do.

Just then Sue heard a loud humming coming from the air. Standing, she looked up and down the empty street. There wasn't even so much as a breeze to blow the trash around. She could hear distant footsteps of someone running down a nearby street, but they faded quickly away. She looked up to the gray sky, the dull sunlight unable to break through the heavy cover of clouds. It was then that she saw the streetlamp near her grow soft and begin to bend, its heavy lamp hitting the street, the glass shattering in thick, uneven shards. Another streetlamp across the street did the same, wilting like a flower. Soon all the streetlamps were falling as if they were melting in the sun. She looked toward the place of worship, on the far side of the crash site, and saw people running inside, shutting the heavy wooden doors behind them.

Sue heard a loud *pop* and turned back to see an electric sign above a storefront suddenly light up and glow. It burned so brightly that it blew out its bulbs before falling heavily onto the street. It was then that she saw him, hovering in the air above them. Victor on the board, still shining, still powerful. Still deadly.

Victor floated just above the Surfer, who was still leaning against the building. His dull, tarnished skin looked even worse next to the radiant glow of Victor and the board. The Surfer looked up at Victor, horrified by the sight of him. He had a sudden awareness that this was how the others had seen him—all the other people on all the other worlds. This was what they saw before their planet was destroyed.

Victor locked eyes with the Surfer. *This pathetic being didn't deserve the power the board granted*, he thought. The Surfer wasn't strong enough to handle such a gift. Victor, however, was. It was destiny, he thought, to be reborn by destroying the very thing that had once ripped him apart molecule by molecule and left him to rot deep within a cave of ice. "You should have taken me up on my offer," Victor said coldly. It would have saved them both a lot of trouble.

Victor extended his hand into the air. Silver matter rippled on the surface of the board near his feet and started working its way up through Victor's body, a traveling motion of waves that undulated up his side and ended in the palm of his hand. The silver matter congealed there before elongating, growing and thinning, taking the shape of a long silver spear. Victor cocked his arm, ready to unleash his new weapon on the Surfer. He wanted to pierce him through and be done with this, thereby taking sole ownership of the board.

Suddenly a force field surrounded him. Victor looked over to see Sue running toward the Surfer, her hand extended before her, keeping the field intact. Her eyes burned holes in Victor as she tried to constrict the field around him. He could feel it cutting into the molecules of air surrounding his metallic skin.

He gave her an evil smile. "Sorry, Susan," he said, his voice low and deep. "Not this time." With one gesture from his free hand the field was hurled back at Sue. She let out a yelp as the energy hit her like a ton of bricks, knocking her off her feet.

Sue fell to the ground, the Surfer reaching out his arm in a futile, instinctive reaction to catch her. How pathetic. The power of the board imbued Victor with a lethal silver glow, as he aimed the point of the spear directly at the Surfer's head. Nothing would survive its deadly touch—even this creature whom Victor once thought all-powerful.

A few blocks away, Reed was limping down a side street with Ben and Johnny. They had found one another quickly, Reed using his elongated torso to stretch up into the air and follow the smoke given off by Ben's crashed jet. Reed had led them to the outskirts of Shanghai, where he thought he spied another smoke trail near a large temple not far from the center of the city. Reed was concerned about Sue, but also fearful of another encounter with Victor. Nothing in their arsenal could match the power of the board. Not one of them had enough power to stop him.

Reed stretched out his hand, causing Ben and Johnny to stop dead in their tracks. Reed cocked his head; he thought he heard the sound of an explosion. It was followed by a loud crash of glass and metal. Instinctively, all three of them sped toward the sound of the fight.

They rounded a corner just in time to see Victor hovering in the air on his board above the figure of the Silver Surfer. Reed scanned the street looking for Sue until finally he saw her, lying a few feet from the Surfer. *Thank God*, Reed thought. *We're not too late. She's still alive.*

Sue pulled her body across the street, crawling over the pavement toward the cornered Surfer. Her brown eyes were wild and determined. She had to reach him. Everything in her body told her this, and she felt every muscle ache and strain in her attempt to make it to him. But she was too late. Victor brought his arm back, preparing to unleash the fatal spear.

It was like Sue witnessed the action in slow motion. She saw Victor throw his arm forward, saw the spear leave his hand and take to the air. She could sense its overwhelming power, its direct connection to the board, a weapon born out of the same power that could destroy entire worlds. The tip of the spear shone brightly even in the overcast light of the morning. The spear parted the air as it made its way toward the Surfer. Sue screamed "No!" and, using the last of her energy, threw her body directly in front of the wounded silver being. Directly in front of the spear.

The powerful weapon impaled her torso. She felt a rush of air, like she had taken a long, deep breath, and then she felt nothing. She crumpled to the ground like a ruined flower.

Reed stopped breathing when he saw the silver spear pierce the woman he loved. "Sue!" he yelled.

He could only imagine what Johnny felt at the sight of his sister falling to the street, the spear sticking out of her body at a perfect right angle. "*No!*" Johnny screamed.

Victor's eyes grew wide when he saw the spear hit not its target but the woman he'd once loved, the woman who'd once made him feel human. He let out a deep growl and took to the air, letting the board take him higher and higher, away from the sight of it.

The fool Johnny Storm decided to pursue. A fatal mistake, to be sure.

With a mere swipe of his hand, Doom's cosmic power sent the insect flying back toward the ground, right where he belonged with all the other insignificant mortals. He saw Storm crash into the street below . . . yet still alive somehow, even as his doltish rocky companion made his way over to him to see if Victor had left him in one piece.

Reed rushed to Sue's side, shock and fear pulsing through his body. He gathered her in his arms, cradling her head gently, mindful of the deep, penetrating wound in her chest. The entire front of her uniform was covered in blood. Her blood.

Once Victor was out of range the spear disintegrated, but Sue's wound did not. She continued to bleed out onto the empty Shanghai street, a bright silk scarf still clutched in her hand. It took a moment for her to let it go.

Her beautiful brown eyes were round and moist, glassy as marbles. They struggled to focus until she saw Reed, holding her close and trying to keep her warm against the onset of shock.

"Reed," she said, drawing the word out in a long exhale. "Where's Victor?"

Reed welled up with tears at the sound of her frail, weakened voice. "Don't try to talk," he said. He was unable to bear the sight of her, his eyes pleading with her to stop. To breathe. To hold on.

"You have to find a way to get the board," she said.

"I can't. I . . ." Reed let out a sob. "I don't know how."

"Listen to me . . . you can do this . . . it's who you are. It's why you're here . . ." She smiled lovingly at him, her eyes memorizing his face in one last, long look. "It's why I love you." As soon as the last word left her lips she started to tremble, wincing in pain. A curtain fell over her features, taking her away from him. Reed held her tightly as her body continued to shake. A thin line of blood escaped from the corner of her mouth and ran down onto the dirty street beneath her.

Suddenly the street filled with darkness. The gray morning turned into night, as if the sun had disappeared. A loud, horrible rumbling came from the sky, followed by shattering blasts of thunder and lightning. Strong winds appeared, blowing trash and one long silk scarf down the street, twisting it into the air and taking it away. Reed held on to Sue tightly, feeling the last of her body's warmth give way to the cold blasts of air.

The Surfer, holding on to the building for support, rose from the ground. His dull face was racked with anguish, after watching the beautiful human protect him. As her life bled into the street he stared at the others around him. The man cradling her, bent over in sadness. The young one, no longer made of flames, his face contorted with grief. And the powerful one, made of rocks, large and so strong but still useless in the face of the coming power. The Surfer looked up to the dark sky, felt the Earth tremble beneath him in complaint. He had seen this before. He had caused this to happen.

"It is here," he intoned, unable to mask the sadness in his voice.

19

THE VERY ATMOSPHERE OF THE EARTH SEEMED TO tremble. The thick formations of clouds parted and dissipated as it arrived, dropping down through the atmosphere without thought to the heat, fire, and gases burning all around it. The Destroyer moved closer and closer to the surface of the planet. It blotted out the sun. It dropped the temperature of the planet by tens of degrees. The very core of the Earth quickened and panicked, sensing its end was near.

Gah Lak Tus arrived in the air over the Pacific seaboard. The swirling vortex of organic matter and energy was unlike anything the world had ever seen. It held the power of more than a thousand hurricanes and yet took on the appearance of one, its layers and layers of quickly turning wind and air masking the destructive energy that lay at its center.

Down below, on a deserted, windy street in the Shanghai market district, the Fantastic Four remained motionless. The sudden and violent change in the weather surrounded them. The strong winds were ripping wooden roofs and structures apart, casting chunks and beams of timber into the air. The dark sky was menacing, filled with the energy and thundering clouds that had obliterated the sun. Large fingers of lightning could be seen sporadically lighting the horizon. Bits of hail fell, stirred by the cold winds. The ground beneath them started to crack, opening large, gaping wounds in the middle of the street that would lead to the core of the planet.

If Reed Richards had ever imagined what the end of the world would look like, it was there in the dying landscape before him. He watched buildings reduced to rubble in seconds, trees wilting and dying in less than that. The entire world seemed to creak and groan, a sharp dagger dangling just over its pumping heart. As a man of science, the logistics of what he was seeing were incomprehensible. Science and logic failed him. He was flooded with a completely emotional response.

And yet none of it mattered. Beyond the horrors around him, his world was ending on a much more intimate scale, there in his two arms. The body of the woman he loved was cradled there, drawing shallow, weak breaths, fading in and out of his vision. He held her close, trying to protect her from the debris falling all around them. Ben provided some cover, shielding them from the flying wreckage of the market stalls, so they could be alone. Alone as the world ended.

Reed held Sue close, trying to keep her long blowing hair away from her face. Her brow furrowed every few seconds as she winced at the pain from her injuries. Reed kept pressure on the large wound but he knew it wasn't enough. She had lost too much blood. A soft moan escaped from her mouth. Her eyes remained shut. *Better that she not see what's happening,* Reed thought. It wouldn't be long now.

As Reed held her, the world falling to pieces around them, his mind took him back through their years together: the first time he spotted Sue at MIT, the first time he showed her the view from the Baxter Building, the vision of her in her wedding dress. That perfect dress. Before he messed everything up, putting that sensor on the roof. Before the Surfer arrived and all hell broke loose. But they had prevailed. They had defeated the Surfer, using Reed's mind and the science he was so willing to give up now.

Sue's last words rushed through his mind then. *You can do this. It's who you are. It's why you're here.* She was right. He couldn't let her life end this way, bleeding on a street as the entire planet was destroyed. He had to control his emotions now, and use more than just science. And he couldn't do it alone. He had to draw on the courage of the group. They could no longer be bystanders, observing the end of the world. They had to be heroes.

Reed motioned for Ben and a stricken Johnny to come closer. Reed's mind was racing with ideas as he tried to form a plan. "Victor's got to have a tachyon pulse emitter linking him to the board," Reed said, explaining how Victor was controlling the powerful silver weapon. "It must be built into his armor. We take it out, and we can separate him from the board."

Johnny took his eyes off his sister long enough to speak. "He's too strong for me."

Ben's expression grew grim. "I could whale on him, if I could get close enough. But he'd see me comin' a mile away."

"It would take all of us . . ." Reed began, until the answer hit him like a thousand lightbulbs going on in his mind. "Or one of us."

Perhaps he had been missing the point all along. The Surfer, this intergalactic being, saw the entire planet, miraculous and complete, a living system of organic matter all connected together. One touch altered Johnny's powers, switching them with the others. Not just any of the others, but the ones closest to him. *His family*. He was able to share their powers, feel what it was like to be them, and bask in the abilities that only they themselves could know. *He was connected to them*. It wasn't a side effect from the Surfer. *It was a gift*.

Ben and Johnny looked perplexed, even as Reed's expression was renewed and determined, hopeful. "Ben, come closer. Johnny, you too." Reed grabbed Sue's hand in his own, reaching out for the space between them. Ben and Johnny joined in, the four hands

234

stacking on top of one another in close and direct contact, a sign of solidarity and strength.

The transformation began just like it had before. Johnny's contact with the other members of the group caused the creation of a large, swirling cloud, alight with energy and cosmic dust. The light grew out from him, enveloping the entire street, the cloud pulsing and growing, lighting up the darkness, a sudden and new candle in the increasingly dark and dangerous world.

Victor Von Doom reveled in the presence of chaos. He floated gracefully in the air, sturdy atop the silver board, while the world went to hell around him. Hovering over the center of Shanghai he watched the crowded, densely populated area crack and crumble. Pieces of buildings and a few cars twirled in the air, caught on the violent currents all around him, while he stood calmly upon the board. Lightning crashed down from the heavy batch of thick clouds, causing fires in the forests surrounding the city. Entire blocks of buildings were either aflame or brought to ruin, tumbling in upon themselves. Lakes were stirred to a rolling boil and began to give off steam, killing every living thing within them as they evaporated from the liquefying of the earth's center. The surge of power within the board that accompanied the arrival of the Destroyer was tremendous. Victor let his eyes roll back in his head, feeling the euphoria overtake his body completely. It was a divine experience, the amount of power and strength surging through him, as the Earth gave up its final resistance. The power of death was sublime.

His body trembled with delight as constant, rabid laughter spilled from his mouth. He watched a mountain crumble into dirt. He saw the craters begin to glow, opening like hungry mouths, eager to begin streaming the molten core of the earth into the Destroyer that now sat high in the sky, just inside the planet's atmosphere. Victor's eyes grew wide as he witnessed the sanctity not of creation, but of destruction.

Calm settled around Victor, the board protecting him from the chaos all around him. The wind did little more than whisper to him, tiny voices telling him he was safe. But suddenly a different voice whispered in his ear. He thought his mind was playing tricks on him, but the voice was familiar. Confident and cocky at the same time.

The voice grew louder and he realized it was the voice of Johnny Storm. He shook his head, trying to dispel it, swatting his hand at the air like he would swat a fly. The voice grew louder until he heard not just whispers but actual words.

"To quote a friend of mine . . ." he heard, and turned around to see Johnny materialize in front of him. "It's clobberin' time!"

As Johnny appeared, Victor saw that his person had

changed: His body appeared to be made of rock, but his trim frame still burned with living fire. Johnny drew back his now large fist and pounded Victor in the face with its rocky power. Victor went flying back from the blow, across the vast expanse of sky. Johnny stretched out his other fist, reaching through the torrents of wind and hail, and pulled Victor back to him. Johnny then hit him again, this time with a blow that would have leveled a building.

Victor flew backward once again, reeling from the tremendous punch, which knocked him across the dark and foreboding skyline toward the center of Shanghai. He crashed directly into a large billboard, its face imploding from the sudden and powerful impact before falling to the street many stories below.

Victor quickly recovered from the blow, summoning up his strength through the surfboard, and flew toward Johnny. He raised his hands toward a large office building, pulling pieces from it to hurl at the Human Torch. One by one large hunks of glass and concrete flew at Johnny like deadly, heavy missiles. Johnny flew evasively around them, but one chunk caught him squarely in the chest, throwing him backward. Johnny flew into the side of a building, smashing through layers of glass and rubble, falling through the wreckage and ending up on its other side. Victor laughed as he saw Johnny disappear into the tangle of debris.

Johnny regained his balance and threw himself back

toward Victor like a human spear made of fire. He burned his flames as strongly as he could; he was surrounded by an aura of bright reds and oranges. Victor focused for a moment and raised his hands, harnessing the strong air currents around him and using them to send Johnny up and over him. The strong rush of air caught Johnny off guard and he went flying uselessly over Victor, careening backward into the heavy air. As he flew away from Victor, Johnny passed a large antenna bolted to the roof of a building, still intact. He elongated his arm, stretching out his hand to reach it. He grabbed the metal antenna with a fist made of rock and swung back around, ricocheting through the air, using his momentum to propel himself toward Victor and the board.

Johnny concentrated and formed a fireball of rock in his hand. He hurled it at Victor, the weight of the rock carrying it through the powerful winds toward its target. Victor deflected it, forcing the air to take it far up and safely away from him. Victor smirked at Johnny, his face a mask of derision. *You can't touch me, kid,* he thought, eager to destroy Johnny the way he had his sister.

Johnny caught Victor's look and simmered with anger. Determination filled of his entire body. He thought of his sister down on the ground, his face contorting in pain. *She'd want to be here for this,* he told himself. *So it's only right that she gets to finish it.*

Johnny clenched his fists and once again aimed himself at Victor. His body was rigid and severe. He dove directly through the powerful winds and currents, ignoring their fury and focusing solely on Victor. His fists drew tighter and his heart raced. Victor was only a few feet away. This would be over soon.

Victor stood strongly on top of the board, steeling himself for Johnny's attack. He was growing impatient with the boy's futile determination. *Can he not see what is happening all around us?* Victor thought. He did not want to be distracted from the main show: watching the destroyer consume this pathetic little planet. He eyed Johnny's darting form and prepared to finish this once and for all. *No more games*, Victor thought. *No more mercy.*

Suddenly Johnny disappeared. A hint of confusion formed in Victor's brain as he scanned the dark, violent sky, wondering if the boy had been taken up in the storm. Victor's eyes narrowed as he searched the dark clouds and pulsating energy fields. He saw nothing. He scanned the ruined streets below, looking for movement among the cracked streets and twisted debris on the ground. Again, nothing. *Where the hell did he go?* Victor thought.

Just then Victor's body convulsed, as if he was caught up in a seizure. He lost control of his arms, and they were drawn in tightly to his sides. He legs clamped together as if caught in a vise. Standing alone on the board, hovering in midair, Victor froze as he realized he couldn't move an inch.

Johnny's rocky form rematerialized as he cast off his sister's power of invisibility, stretching his body to cover Victor entirely. Johnny used Reed's elasticity to engulf Victor like a rubber coating, shrouding him from head to toe. Victor struggled as if in a straitjacket, but Johnny's rocky hide was too dense and heavy to lift. Using the powers of his friends to immobilize Victor, Johnny turned to the one power he knew best: his own. He ignited his thinly stretched and rocky body, covering Victor with his living flame. He burned strong and bright, flaming as hard and fast as he could. Johnny thought of his sister's face as he pushed himself to the limit, approaching supernova. He burned a hole in the surrounding darkness as Victor screamed and writhed in his incendiary grip.

The metallic armor smoked and singed from Johnny's assault. Burning from the intense heat. Victor continued to struggle and toss about but Johnny kept him locked tight in his fiery embrace, bringing Victor down from his high altitude to the airspace just above a series of tall buildings. Victor's limbs scorched and smoked. The tachyon pulse emitter melted into nothing, turning to ash and air, severing Victor's link with the board.

Victor's body went limp as his bond with the board was destroyed. A rush of profound despair assaulted

Victor's entire psyche as he was cast off from his link to the powerful silver weapon. The euphoria faded and the silence of the world returned to him as he lost his connection to the sublime destruction around him.

Johnny heard Ben calling out to him. He looked over to see Ben in his human form, sitting at the controls of a massive construction crane adjacent to a nearby building. Ben had been sitting with Reed and Sue, struggling with his feelings of uselessness as he watched the events around him: the crumbling city, the arrival of the destroyer, the last breaths of the dying Sue. *I can't just sit here*, he'd told himself, running the few blocks to where Johnny was fighting Victor. He spied the large crane and took the wheel.

"Hey, kid," he yelled at Johnny. "Watch out!" Ben threw a few levers on the control panel, swinging a massive bundle of steel girders, still attached to the crane, in Victor's direction. Johnny jumped off Victor at the last second, watching the hurled girders slice through the air straight toward them. They smashed into Victor mercilessly, the screeching sound of metal clashing with metal ringing out as they knocked Victor off the shining silver board and into the air. The thundering impact of the girders knocked Victor immediately unconscious. His limp figure ricocheted through the air before plummeting, landing with a loud splash in the river, the churning waters wild with the Earth's heat. The weight of his armor took him down quickly, his silver skin now scorched and ruined. Victor disappeared into the dark and merciless water.

A few blocks away, Reed continued to hold Sue gently, cradling her in his arms. The violent trembling of the ground was getting worse. The sky appeared darker, Gah Lak Tus now visible to them, a swirling vortex of annihilation and destruction that filled the entire sky.

The Surfer stayed silent, afraid to speak and not knowing what to say. He, too, was to be a casualty of the Destroyer, but he cared little about that. His stoic gaze rested not on the landscape but on the scene before him: the dying woman and the man who loved her. He watched the man try to comfort her, attempting to make her final moments as gentle as possible. He looked away when they started to speak because it was too painful to witness.

"Just relax," Reed whispered to Sue, touching her face. "Think about how our life's going to be. A nice house in the country. Kids playing in the yard." His voice caught in his throat as he wiped a tear from his eye.

Sue opened her eyes and looked up at him. She smiled slowly. "That sounds so nice," she said, the words barely able to leave her lips. She reached up to touch his face but her hand stopped in midair. Her fingers trembled a bit before the hand fell back to her wet, bloody chest, lifeless.

Reed kept repeating her name, his voice breaking loudly, as he clutched her to his chest. His body wracked with sobs as he realized she was gone.

20

JOHNNY STORM BRACED HIMSELF AGAINST THE WILD winds raging over the crumbling city of Shanghai. Debris flew across the dark and angry sky. The world seemed to be giving up the last of its riches in the presence of the destroyer: forests ripped up from their soil and flew into the air; skyscrapers fell like houses made of playing cards, revealing their bare metal skeletons; lakes and rivers bubbled and dried up, the last of their waters steamed away. The river, which had just consumed Victor Von Doom, lay roiling just beneath Johnny's flaming, hovering form, another scar on a devastated landscape. The sight of the apocalyptic skyline filled Johnny with trepidation and fear. He had never seen anything like it before. He looked up at the massive vortex of energy and power now clearly visible and taking up much of the air in his sight line. Gah Lak Tus was here, drawn to this place by the Surfer and his board. They didn't have much time left. He had to get the board back to the group and hope the Surfer could stop this madness.

Johnny grabbed the shining silver board and felt

his fingers tingle from its touch. Its power was extraordinary, even with both of its previous riders defeated and out of commission. *It must be the Destroyer*, Johnny thought. It didn't matter who rode the board; its destructive connection to the massive, living vortex remained undiminished.

Johnny fought his way through the violent winds, pushing himself against the near-catastrophic sky. He burned his flames higher, hoping the surrounding fire would shield him from the worst of the flying debris. Half the city seemed to be in the air with him; he dodged various pieces of timber and metal, making his way through the carnage all around him. It wasn't long until he spied the familiar market street and saw the others crouched in the doorway of a building, one of the few still left intact. He raced down to them, turning off his flames as soon as his feet touched the unstable ground. He ran over to the others, noticing that Ben and Reed were still hovering over his sister. "I got it," Johnny said excitedly, holding up the shining board. The others barely seemed to notice his arrival. He dropped the board and grabbed their shoulders, the direct contact once again triggering the massive display of light and energy that signaled the switching of their special powers. Johnny felt the energy surging through him as it had before, but this time something felt different. The connection felt a bit off, as if something was missing.

As soon as the light faded he noticed the difference in the group. Ben, his rocky visage once again in place, still looked crestfallen, his massive shoulders hunched and low. Reed had barely noticed Johnny's arrival and Johnny could now see him clutching Sue, weeping openly. His sister had yet to stir, and he saw the large wound covering her chest. *No*, he thought suddenly.

"*Sue?!*" he yelled. But she did not move. Johnny fell to his knees, tears forming in his eyes. It was then that he knew his sister was dead.

"I'm sorry, kid," Ben said softly, but Johnny couldn't hear him. He was already flooded with grief, and he couldn't help the images that flew into his mind: happy times from their childhood together; her bright, soft face always patient, even when she was angry with his hotheaded personality; the image of her standing at the Baxter Building, looking radiant in her beautiful wedding dress, her head surrounded by delicate lace. All the things he never said to her crashed into him then and formed a lump in his throat. He would never have the chance to say them to her, or find a way to make up for any of it. She was gone.

The Surfer stayed silent, watching the vivid display of grief around him. His eyes remained deep pools of dull silver, but began to leak tears. He had never been so close to the destruction he was connected to, had never seen up close what havoc the presence of Gah

Lak Tus caused. His thoughts had always been about his own home, the loved ones he left behind; he'd never lingered on the ones who suffered under his touch. But here it was, painfully displayed before him: the dead body of the woman who saved him, the grieving figures of her friends and loved ones who had also tried to protect him. The Surfer struggled with the realization that their futile gestures amounted to nothing beyond their own grief. Their actions had no effect on the arrival of Gah Lak Tus and the destruction of their planet.

The sky grew darker around them, shades of gray turning into swaths of deep purple and black. Large meteors crashed into the ground, shaking the street and filling the air with rock and dust. The Surfer could feel the energy in the Earth beneath him start to rumble and give way as the Destroyer prepared to feast on the planet's core. Somewhere, he knew, bright spires of molten rock were emanating from the craters he'd made and feeding the great beast. It wouldn't be long now before this planet, like so many others before it, would be consumed.

The Surfer stood, pulling his injured body up against the corner of the crumbling building. He looked up to watch the roof of the structure fly off and up into the dark, swirling air. The Earth boomed with sound as more meteors hit its surface, cracking it like an egg. The Surfer limped over and grabbed the glowing board that Johnny had so carelessly tossed aside. As soon as he made direct contact with it, light grew from its source and covered him entirely. The Surfer's leg healed instantly and his body regained its bright, silver gleam. He appeared as he was before. Ben, Johnny, and Reed could feel the heat of the energy on their faces, a small burst of warmth in the thickening and cool air. With his power returned, the Surfer once again appeared radiant, glowing, otherworldly.

Reed looked up from Sue's lifeless body to see the Surfer returned to his power. Part of him hated the silver figure, for it was his arrival here that had led to all of this. But the Surfer was the only one who could draw the Destroyer away from the planet. As much as Reed hated to admit it, they needed the Surfer. They needed him to leave.

The Destroyer loomed larger than before, taking up the entire sky with its dark power. It was almost close enough now, close enough to feed on the planet's core.

"You've got to go now," Reed said, yelling over the sound of the wind.

"Not yet," the Surfer said. He walked out into the street clutching the board. He surveyed the broken landscape and watched the sky carry pieces of the planet away. Death was all around him, just like it always was. But this time the price was too high. The Surfer could not, would not, expose this place to any more loss. The Surfer turned back to Reed. "You will not suffer my fate. Step away," he said, motioning Reed and the others away from Sue's lifeless body. Reed laid her gently on the ground, pulling the grieving Johnny and Ben away from her.

The Surfer raised his hands into the air. He closed his eyes, suddenly lost in concentration. Even with the world falling to pieces around him, the Surfer radiated a sense of pure serenity, like a safe haven in the overwhelming storm. Reed watched him wordlessly, once again transfixed by the ethereal calm of the silver being. The Surfer's hands began to pulse and glow, a shining beacon against the dark sky. The light grew brighter and brighter, increasing to a radiance none of them had ever seen before. It almost hurt to look at it, but no one in the group could turn away.

The Surfer opened his eyes quickly, locking them on the lifeless figure of Susan Storm. From his deeply pooled eyes came rays of silver light that lashed out across the air, alive like snakes, enveloping her in their glow. It looked as if the Surfer had turned himself inside out and was unleashing the radiant power that lived inside of him, transferring his very essence onto her lifeless form. Reed watched the incredible display of power, his eyes growing wide as Sue's physical body broke apart on a molecular level, the atoms reduced to small, glowing motes of dust. The motes danced and pulsed before coming back together in a round ball of pure, glowing energy. The energy stretched out into the form of a woman as the molecules reverted to the shape of Susan Storm. Reed watched her materialize in front of him, her body once again resting on the trembling street. Her wound was gone. Her eyes fluttered and remained closed but her chest moved with breath, her skin once again pink and warm and filled with life.

The Surfer collapsed to the street, his radiant skin simmering down to a dull glow. His body showed signs of the strain and Ben ran to his side to hold the silver figure up. Ben could feel the Surfer lean on him, exhausted.

Reed rushed to Sue's side, taking her in his arms, making sure her breathing was regular and even. He wiped a long stand of hair from her face and caressed her warm cheek. He heard the Surfer's deep and wavering voice say, "Life and death are but different forms of energy."

Reed let grateful tears stream down his cheeks. "Thank you," he said to the Surfer, once again holding the woman he loved.

The Surfer regained his composure quickly, drawing up his strength and leaving Ben's side. His silver skin was radiant and glowing with power, his face stoic and resolute. He stood on his board and hovered over the Four. He took a final look at those below him. "Savor each moment with her," he told Reed before taking to the air.

The Surfer sped up into the sky, the violent winds swirling all around him. He struggled to rise higher, the board no longer able to protect him from the catastrophe occurring around him. The Surfer summoned all of his might to whisk himself higher and higher into the maelstrom above the surface of the planet.

But he couldn't do it. The presence of the Destroyer was too intense, the atmosphere too unstable, the end too near. He fought against the gale-force winds and small hurricanes that cracked through the sky. The Surfer flipped and struggled against them all, caught in the heavy riptides of air all around him. He focused his mind, trying to rise higher. He had to break though the chaos if he was ever to punch through the atmosphere and draw Gah Lak Tus away from the planet.

Suddenly he shot up through the air, bursting through the maddening winds swirling around him. He broke free of the riptides and sped into the upper reaches of the atmosphere. He looked back and saw the Human Torch, covered in living flame, gripping the back of his board and propelling them both toward the heavens. The powerful flame acted like a booster rocket, taking them through the rough winds and debris. The dark sky fell away, lightening a bit before the beginnings of outer space again became visible.

A strong sense of déjà vu overcame Johnny as he propelled them away from the planet's surface. He had been here with the Surfer before, not that long ago. Their previous fight had taken them to the highest reaches of Earth's atmosphere as Johnny had struggled with the feelings of isolation that came with a bird's-eye-view of the planet. It looked different to him now. The planet, now under siege, looked vulnerable and precious, something to protect and defend. His hands, still connected to the powerful board, felt these feelings surge within him just as the flames on his fingers began to extinguish. The lack of oxygen at such a high altitude began to diminish the flames all over his body. "Okay," Johnny said to the Surfer. "That's it for me. From here on out, you're golden! I mean . . . silver. Whatever." Johnny saw the Surfer's eyes meet his just as his hand that touched the board began to tingle. Johnny gave the Surfer a final push and watched him rocket out of the Earth's atmosphere.

Johnny reversed his course and sped back down toward the surface of the planet, his flames returning to strength in the oxygen-rich atmosphere. Upon re-entry, he was battered about by the storm of meteors and debris, though his flames burned up and shielded him from the largest bits of detritus. He ricocheted off them, caroming down to the surface of the planet.

Just then, a barrage of large boulders and wreckage caught in a twister headed straight for him. At this speed, Johnny didn't have time to maneuver or turn. He burned brighter and closed his eyes, bracing for the painful impact.

Back down on the surface of the planet, things continued to tremble and shake. The winds blew up large amounts of dust that clouded the horizon. There was no sun, and no light. Reed tried to shelter Sue, who was still weak but breathing. Ben covered them both, his thick, rocky hide their only protection from the violence around them. Nothing had changed since the Surfer's departure. The air remained dark, heavy, and thick. The devastation around them was covered by the dust storms, but they could hear the cacophony of loud crashes and collisions around them. "Why isn't it working?" Ben yelled against the onslaught, bracing himself as more debris slammed into his back.

Reed tried to close himself off from the destruction around them. "We were too late," he said sadly, drawing Sue closer to him.

"Then this is it," Ben replied, suddenly thinking of Alicia. "This is the end." Ben huddled closer to Reed and Sue, prepared to protect them as long as he could, until the very end. A loud *boom* made them all start, and a large crack opened in the Earth near them. Ben could feel the steam escaping from the large hole and scalding his thick leg, the planet preparing to bleed out its core into the open air. He hoped that the end would be swift and that his rocky form might shield his friends from some of the pain. He shut his eyes tightly, whispering a prayer. The Earth shuddered and shook beneath them, tossing Reed against Ben in a final violent display. Reed shut his eyes, gripping Sue to his chest.

And then suddenly, the shaking stopped.

High above the Earth's atmosphere, the Silver Surfer burst through the swirling, powerful essence of Gah Lak Tus.

No more of this, thought the Surfer. *Not this world. Not her.*

For this first time in the Surfer's memory, Gah Lak Tus was taken off guard. He could feel it penetrating his thoughts, attempting to mine some semblance of reason for its herald's transgression, this unexpected interruption of its feeding.

What then would be the price of Norrin Radd's insubordination?

The Silver Surfer raced away from the lonely blue planet, his merciless cosmic overlord eager to pursue.

The chaos around the Fantastic Four grew quiet. The wind died down, and the massive amounts of dust in the air fell in thick clusters to the ground. The dark atmosphere around them lifted, letting little cracks of light break through the cloud cover. The cracks of light grew wider, brighter, forming a glow on the horizon. Ben looked up to see a flaming spot in the sky, glowing brightly, coming directly toward them. Johnny broke through just as the darkness dissipated and the sun became apparent in the sky behind him. As the smoke and dust cleared away, they all could see the Destroyer pulling away from the Earth, moving at an incredible speed, allowing the gray and charred sky to return to their view.

Johnny landed on the ground near them, his arrival kicking up a cloud of dust. He turned off his flames and ran to the others. "He did it," he said, a large grin breaking over his face.

Sue sat up, brushing dirt and dust from her uniform. She looked over at her brother, and then at Reed. "What did I miss?" she asked. Reed smiled and kissed her, pulling her close to him.

Ben stood up, pushing a half-torn rooftop off his back and kicking away some of the debris around them. He walked over to Johnny and patted him on the back. "Nice work, kid," he said.

"Thanks," Johnny said, his shoulder caving under Ben's heavy touch. Johnny suddenly flinched, remembering his ability to switch powers with the others. But the direct contact had no effect. "Hey," he said. "I'm not changing! I'm cured."

Ben smiled. "It must have been your quality time with Norbert . . ." he said.

Johnny remembered the strange tingling in his hands just before he'd pushed the Surfer off toward space. He kept touching Ben all over, making sure the ability to switch powers had finally left him. "Norrin," Johnny replied.

"Okay," Ben said, pushing Johnny back. "Now you're making me uncomfortable."

Reed was oblivious to Johnny and Ben's interaction, focusing his attention solely on Sue. She looked tired but still beautiful. He couldn't believe he had almost lost her. He vowed to himself that he would never let that happen again. He grasped her hand and held it tightly.

"So I guess it's all over, huh?" said Ben from behind him. "Now you can go start your new life."

"No," replied Reed.

"No?"

"No," Sue parroted.

"Yes!" Johnny shouted, ecstatic.

"If it wasn't for us," explained Reed, "the whole world would be gone now. What are we going to do during the next crisis?"

"We can't run and hide from the people we need to protect," said Sue, looking at Reed with love. "It's who we are."

It's who we are.

"Exactly!" said Johnny. "I was going to say that!"

Ben still looked befuddled. "But what about having a normal life—a *family*?"

Reed smiled at his words. "Who says you have to be normal to have a family?"

Besides . . ." said Sue. "We already *are* a family."

She reached her hand out to her brother, who quickly walked to her side. They placed their joined hands out, one over the other, Ben joined in, his huge fist enveloping them both. They all looked at Reed, their leader, who soon followed suit, placing his hand over Ben's. Reed knew that the team had been stretched to the breaking point. But they'd recovered, just like they always did. They had saved the planet, and nothing in this world or any other would ever tear them apart again.

"You up for another media circus wedding?" asked Sue, a small smile on her face. "Sixth time's the charm."

Reed couldn't help grinning. "No. I've got a better idea."

EPILOGUE

THE EARLY AFTERNOON WAS CALM, SUNNY, AND BRIGHT. The sun had returned to its place in the sky and was warming the blue horizon with its unblinking stare. A gentle breeze wafted through the Japanese garden, stirring the manicured trees and shrubs. Tufted moss cascaded down a small incline to the left of a wooden pergola, which was adorned with long drapes of fine silk. To the right sat a small pond, with large water lilies floating peacefully on its surface. Reed surveyed the landscape and drew a deep breath of clean, fresh air. It was hard for him to believe that a serene landscape such as this had almost been lost. But with its preservation came a sense of renewal, for him and for the others.

He looked over to see Susan standing next to a stone lantern near a large blooming tree. One of the monks here told Reed that the crimson colors of the changing Japanese maple tree were meant to create awareness of the passage of time. Reed had nodded serenely to the kind monk, for that was something they all seemed to understand better now, after almost losing so much.

Susan gave Reed a warm smile and started walking toward him. She wore a simple cotton dress, its white fabric glowing in the radiant daylight. A water lily adorned her blond hair, a last-minute gift from a passing monk who'd been looking after the garden. She walked the simple path to join Reed under the pergola, passing Johnny, Ben, Alicia, and a few other close friends on the way. Susan wanted a simple ceremony, one held far away from the eyes of the world. As she looked out at the beautiful garden she felt protected by the lush landscape, grateful to be here.

Ben Grimm stood watching Susan join Reed under the pergola. He held Alicia close to him, as close as his large, rocky frame would allow. He realized now how much he loved her, and how fleeting their time together could be. Ben wanted to make the most of it, in any way he could. "I've got something for you," he whispered to Alicia. He pulled out a silver key on a long chain and placed it in the palm of her hand. "You're going to need it if you're moving in." Alicia felt the cool metal in her cupped hand. She smiled and hugged him.

Their moment together was interrupted by the voice of the minister. "Dearly beloved, we are gathered here today . . ." The minister barely finished the introduction before a crisp beeping filled the air. Reed started at the sound before realizing it was the alarm on his PDA going off. He grabbed the device from his pocket and

259

looked sheepishly at Sue. Her face showed no anger, only concern.

"What is it?" she asked.

Reed scanned the small screen of his PDA. A frown formed on his face. "There's some kind of giant creature attacking Paris."

Johnny clenched his fists, ready for a fight. "Oh, boy," he said with excitement. "That's a biggie." He raised his eyebrows at his sister, as if asking for permission.

Sue smiled at her brother and then turned to the minister. "Can you skip to the end?"

The minister, obviously flummoxed by the turn of events, started to stutter. "Uh, the love these two share—"

"No," Reed interrupted, "the very end!"

"I now pronounce you man and wife!" the minister blurted out.

Reed turned to his bride and smiled. Sue returned the smile and leaned in for their first kiss as husband and wife. After the intimate moment, Sue pulled back quickly. Her face showed that she was all business. "Okay, that's it. Let's go!"

Reed, Sue, Ben, and Johnny raced out of the Japanese gardens, past the changing maple tree and stone garden, past the pond with the gentle water lilies floating on its surface, past the raked sand garden, to the front of the temple. There stood Reed's refurbished jet, all in one piece, now affectionately known to the group as the Fantasticar, polished and shining in the afternoon sunlight. They all jumped in together and Reed revved up the enhanced engines. He pulled the jet up into the pale blue sky, careful not to damage the JUST MARRIED banner on its side as a trail of noisy tin cans followed them up into the air.

ABOUT THE AUTHOR

DANIEL JOSEPHS is a pseudonym for a notable writer and editor who has worked in various aspects of the publishing industry for more than fifteen years. He currently resides in Los Angeles.